PHANTOM FEAR

PHANTOM FEAR
Pete Johnson

Corgi Yearling Books

PHANTOM FEAR
A CORGI YEARLING BOOK : 978 0 440 86690 9

First published in Great Britain as separate editions by Corgi Yearling
an imprint of Random House Children's Books

MY FRIEND'S A WEREWOLF first published 1997
THE PHANTOM THIEF first published 1998

This edition published 2005

3 5 7 9 10 8 6 4 2

Papers used by Random House Children's Books are natural, recyclable
products made from wood grown in sustainable forests. The manufacturing
processes conform to the environmental regulations of the country of origin.

Corgi Yearling Books are published by Random House Children's Books,
61–63 Uxbridge Road, London W5 5SA,
a division of The Random House Group Ltd,
in Australia by Random House Australia (Pty) Ltd,
20 Alfred Street, Milsons Point, Sydney, NSW 2061, Australia,
in New Zealand by Random House New Zealand Ltd,
18 Poland Road, Glenfield, Auckland 10, New Zealand,
and in South Africa by Random House (Pty) Ltd,
Isle of Houghton, Corner of Boundary Road & Carse O'Gowrie,
Houghton 2198, South Africa

THE RANDOM HOUSE GROUP Limited Reg. No. 954009
www.**kids**at**randomhouse**.co.uk

A CIP catalogue record for this book is available from the British Library.

Printed and bound in Great Britain by CPI Antony Rowe, Chippenham, Wiltshire

MY FRIEND'S A WEREWOLF

Illustrated by Peter Dennis

This book is dedicated to:
Jan, Linda, Robin, Harry and Adam,
Bill Bloomfield and Sue Gregory

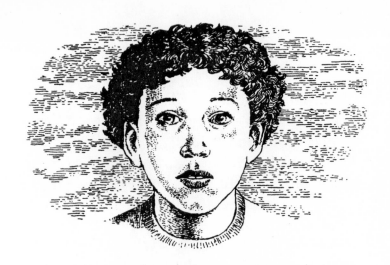

CHAPTER ONE

I thought werewolves only existed in stories and late-night films.

Now I know they are real.

It's an incredible story but I am going to tell you everything.

Then maybe you'll believe too.

I remember exactly when my story started. It was on a Saturday afternoon at the beginning of November. I was pretending to be tidying up my room when actually I was sitting on my bed reading a horror story. It was starting to get dark and

I was just drawing my curtains when the doorbell rang.

'Answer that, love, will you?' called my mum. 'Your dad's not back yet and I'm on the phone to your nan.'

I thumped down the stairs and opened the door to discover this boy I'd never seen in my life before, smiling shyly at me.

'Hello,' he said.

'Hello,' I replied cautiously.

He had curly black hair, very thick eyebrows and enormous dark green eyes. I guessed he was about thirteen, two years older than me.

'I've just moved in next door,' he said.

Mr and Mrs Atkins, who live next door in the end house, have gone to Germany for four years, so they've been letting their house out. The family who were there before never even said hello. They were horrible. We were all glad when they left.

'Do you go to the school down the road, Westcliffe High?' he asked.

I nodded.

'That's where I'm going. I'll be in Mrs Paine's class.'

'Same as me.' What made me think he was older than me? He wasn't especially tall. It must have been those little bits of stubble on his chin.

'So what's Mrs Paine like?' he asked.

'When she's in a bad mood she's a nightmare. And when she tells you off she spits right in your face. I want to say to her: tell me the news, not the weather.'

He started to laugh. 'I'm Simon, by the way.'

'And I'm Kelly.'

'Kelly,' he exclaimed. 'Why, that's a brilliant name.'

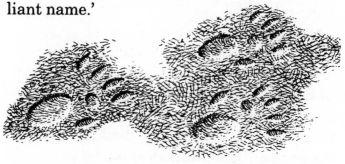

I was really surprised – and pleased – by his reaction, especially as a lot of people say I've got a dog's name and call out 'Here Kelly' and 'Walkies Kelly' when they're trying to be funny.

'Have you got any brothers or sisters?' he asked.

I shook my head.

'Neither have I.'

And I don't know why, but that seemed to create a little bond between us.

I invited him in. He was dressed casually in a blue sports shirt, baggy jeans, Kickers – and black gloves. My eyes kept going back to those black gloves. They had little pads under the fingertips and they just didn't fit in with what he was wearing. Those gloves looked weird somehow.

I took Simon into the kitchen. Muffin, our white cat, was sitting on the table. 'No, Muffin, bad cat,' I said. 'You know you're not supposed to be up there. Come on, down you get.'

To my surprise Muffin starting arching her back and hissing. She was hissing furiously at Simon as if he were her deadliest enemy.

'Muffin, stop that,' I began. But Muffin had already jumped off the table and fled away.

'I'm sorry about that,' I said. 'She's normally much friendlier.'

'She can probably smell my dogs off me. I've got four of them.'

'Four!' I exclaimed.

'Yeah, we had three dogs and now we've just got another one from the animal rescue centre. All my family are just mad about dogs.'

Soon we were chatting away as if we'd known each other for years. My mum and dad introduced themselves to Simon and afterwards pronounced him 'a very nice young lad'. Later Mum also popped next door to say hello, and to find out all the news. She came back saying how Mr and Mrs Doyle had moved here quickly because of Mr Doyle's new job. But if 'things worked out' they would settle in the area.

'Maybe Mr and Mrs Atkins might even sell them the house,' I said excitedly.

Next day Simon invited me round to his house for tea. There were still lots of unpacked boxes in the hallway. I dodged round them and followed Simon into the kitchen. I couldn't believe my eyes. There were platefuls of sausage rolls, sandwiches, cakes, biscuits.

'How many people are you expecting?' I cried.

'Only you,' said Simon.

'But there's enough food here for a party.'

'We just wanted you to feel welcome,' then with a grin he added, 'and we're not going to let you leave until you've eaten it all up.'

'I'll be here for weeks then.'

'That's fine . . . stay as long as you like,' he replied. Then Simon's parents appeared. His dad was very tall and balding while his mum was much smaller but with the same enormous green eyes as Simon. They both kept asking me if I was enjoying myself and seemed really disappointed when I said I couldn't eat any more.

I was about to leave when they insisted I have some hot chocolate, 'for the journey'. I didn't like to point out I was only going next door. Simon's dad brought in a tray of hot chocolate and still more biscuits which I couldn't even look at I was so full. Then Simon's mum asked, 'So, Kelly, is your bedroom at the front or the back of the house?'

I thought this was rather an odd question but I replied, 'At the back.'

At once, Simon's parents leaned forward and stared at me intently. 'Has Simon mentioned we've got four dogs?'

'Yes, I'd really like to see them.'

Simon's mum smiled. 'Well, we kept them away while you were eating, otherwise you wouldn't have got a moment's peace from them . . . At night they sleep outside in their kennel and they're good dogs but they can be a little noisy . . .'

'And we'd hate to think of them keeping you awake,' said Simon's dad.

'Oh, don't worry about that,' I replied at once. 'The neighbours before you were in a band, so I'd hear drums going at two in the morning. My dad said it was a real disgrace and he kept complaining but they never stopped. So after that, a few dogs barking is nothing.'

'Well, if ever they do disturb you, please tell us, won't you?' said Simon's dad.

'Yes, come straight to us,' said Simon's

mum, so firmly it was almost like a command.

I felt a little embarrassed by all this fuss. 'Look, I love dogs myself,' I began.

'Do you?' said Simon eagerly. 'Well, would you like to meet them?'

'Definitely.'

He charged off while his mum called after him: 'Make sure you check they haven't been digging in the mud . . .' She'd hardly finished speaking when three dogs tumbled through the doorway; the two West Highland terriers, yelping excitedly, dived straight on to Mrs Doyle's lap. 'Not both of you up here,' she said, but the dogs ignored her protests and made themselves comfortable. Meanwhile, the brown dog which Simon described as a 'sort of spaniel' circled excitedly around Simon, his tail thumping so hard he nearly sent a vase flying.

Then I spotted a fourth dog. A black labrador wagging his tail rather uncertainly in the doorway.

'That's Plute,' explained Simon. 'We've only had him a little while.'

'His last owners were unkind to him,' said

Simon's mum, 'so he's still a little bit unsure of himself.'

Simon went over to the dog, got down on his knees, put his face right up to Plute and started whispering to him. The dog seemed to be listening to him too. It was as if they were whispering secrets together.

Then Simon got to his feet and at once Plute came over to me. I stroked him gently and then he rolled over on to his back. 'See, he likes you,' cried Simon. 'I told Plute he would.' Later, Simon showed me the kennel in the garden where all the dogs slept.

'But it's huge,' I cried. 'Bigger than my bedroom.' Inside the kennel were all these thick rugs.

'We like our dogs to be comfortable,' said Simon.

'I bet it's funny when you take all four for a walk,' I said.

'It's mad,' laughed Simon, 'especially with Plute. You see, he's got this crazy hobby – he likes to chase cars.'

'Oh no.'

'Yeah, he's always trying to run off so he can go car chasing.' Simon rubbed Plute's head affectionately. 'He's such a nutty dog, that one.'

'Still, he's got a nice lot of space to run around in here,' I said. The whole garden was given over to grass. There were hardly any flowers at all but all round the garden were tall trees and bushes making it seem private and mysterious, almost like a secret garden. I liked that.

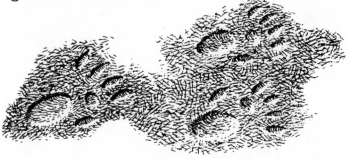

In fact, I felt really happy out there with Simon and all his dogs. Only one thing was bothering me. Simon was wearing those black gloves again. And they just looked so daft. I knew all my friends would think so too. Would he wear them to school tomorrow? He wouldn't be allowed, would he? I couldn't stop staring at them.

Finally, Simon said, 'You don't think

much of my gloves, do you?' He was looking straight at me when he said this.

'Oh no, they're . . .' I gulped hard. 'Well to be honest, I don't like them much,' I admitted finally.

'Nor do I,' said Simon. 'In fact I hate them. But I have to wear them. I've no choice. That's why I've got to take a letter into school tomorrow.' He sighed loudly. 'Shall we go back inside?'

I knew he didn't want to talk about it any more. But I couldn't help wondering what was wrong with his hands. Why did he have to keep them hidden in gloves all the time?

As I was leaving I said, 'I'll call for you for school tomorrow, if you like.'

'That'd be great,' he said eagerly.

'There's another person I call for, Jeff. He lives just up the road. I'm sure you'll like him.'

Simon nodded, then said, 'The dogs have really taken to you.'

'I like them very much too,' I replied.

Simon's face broke into a smile wide enough for two people. 'It's going to be so great us living next door to each other.'

I really agreed with him, then.

CHAPTER TWO

I was still waiting for my cereal to turn the
milk all chocolatey – some days it just takes
ages – when Simon bounded in.

'I'm early, aren't I?' His eyes were
sparkling as if he was going to a party.

'Yes, and you're a bit keen,' I said.

'I know, sorry . . . but Kelly, I just can't
wait.'

'To go to school? You're mad! So what was
your old school like?'

The smile immediately faded off his face.
'It was OK, I guess. But I know this school is

going to be much better.' Then he grinned excitedly at me.

We set off to call for Jeff. I hoped Simon would like him and not judge by appearances. You see, Jeff is very small and very round and known to everyone as 'The Barrel'. When they're picking teams at school he's always the last to be chosen. In fact, no-one actually picks him they just say, 'And you've got The Barrel.'

Yet Simon was really friendly to Jeff, asking him questions about school and his hobbies – well, hobby. Jeff collects superhero comics. But Jeff gave these brief, almost rude answers and all the time spoke in this very flat tone.

We took Simon to the staffroom to see Mrs Paine. Outside the staffroom Jeff hissed, 'What about those black gloves he's wearing. I suppose he thinks he looks cool. Well, I think he looks pathetic.'

'That's so mean,' I replied. 'Simon has to wear those gloves.'

'Why?'

'I don't know exactly.'

'It's probably because his hands look

24

so horrible. I bet they're all greasy and wrinkled and got scabs all over them and . . .'

Jeff was interrupted by the staffroom door opening. Simon appeared. 'Well, she hasn't spat in my face yet,' he said.

I laughed, while Jeff just looked puzzled. Then I introduced Simon to some other people from my form. At first I think he was overwhelmed by this rush of new faces. But soon he was chatting away quite easily.

His arrival was certainly hot news. All day I was asked questions about him. It was good fun actually. Rat-bag Sarah even flounced up to me and said, 'Everyone's talking about you and Simon. Is he your boyfriend or not?'

Of course he wasn't my boyfriend but I wasn't going to tell Sarah that. So I just smiled mysteriously.

'And those gloves. Why? Are they glued to his hands?'

Again I smiled mysteriously. 'That's for me to know and you to find out.'

Sarah didn't like that answer at all. But in the afternoon she ran up to me again, smirking her head off.

'Simon's told me why he has to wear those gloves . . .' She lowered her voice dramatically. 'That fire he was in must have been terrible, mustn't it?'

For a moment I was too shocked to reply, then I said, 'Oh, yes, terrible,' and quickly walked away.

Fancy Simon telling Rat-bag Sarah about the fire he was in – and not me. I was really upset.

Later when I was walking home with Jeff and Simon I said, 'Sarah told me you got your hands burnt in a fire.'

'That's right,' he said shortly. Then he added, 'I really hate talking about it.' He shook his head. 'I had to tell her because she just kept on and on about it. They all did, all . . . except you.' He said those last words as if he were paying me a compliment.

'Sarah is just so nosy . . . I can't stand her actually,' I said.

'I think I like other people a lot more,' replied Simon, looking straight at me. I hoped I wasn't blushing.

Jeff gave this really loud whistle of annoyance; that was all Jeff said until we reached my house. Then he muttered, 'You haven't forgotten you're going to help me with maths homework, have you, Kelly?'

Actually Jeff is practically a genius at maths, so I knew this was his code for, I want to talk to you privately. We were hardly out of Simon's earshot when Jeff was hissing,

'Well, thanks a lot, Kelly. You've practically ignored me all day.'

'No, I haven't,' I replied indignantly.

'Yes you have; at lunchtime you went off with that Simon, leaving me all on my own.'

'I left you in a room full of people,' I cried. 'And I only went off to introduce Simon to some of the football team as he's interested in playing.'

'Oh, is he?' said Jeff sarcastically. 'Well, isn't he just marvellous? I suppose old friends aren't good enough for you now?'

I felt a bit sorry for him – and just the tiniest bit guilty too. 'Oh, Jeff, don't be silly, it's only Simon is new so I have to look after him . . . and you do like him, don't you?'

'No.'

'No?' I was shocked.

'I think he's too good to be true.'

'Oh, what rubbish,' I began.

'There's something weird about him and you'd better be careful living next door to him.'

I gave a strange kind of laugh in reply. 'Well, everyone else likes him.'

Of course it helped that Simon was so brilliant at sports. I'd never seen anyone jump so high in basketball. He was also an amazingly fast runner and very soon was one of the stars of the football team. I stayed behind to cheer him on after school. So did quite a few other girls. Girls were always asking me questions about him and saying things like, 'I think you're so lucky having Simon move next door to you.'

I just smiled when they said that. But secretly I agreed with them. And then came the night of Sarah's fancy-dress party. Everyone from Sarah's form was invited – even me, although I think I was only invited because Sarah's mum and Jeff's mum are always round each other's houses and Sarah knew Jeff wouldn't go without me.

Simon said he had a great idea for his costume but wouldn't tell anyone what it was; he wanted it to be a surprise.

Jeff and I didn't have any ideas at all. Finally on Saturday afternoon we went into town hoping inspiration would strike.

Ever since Jeff and I had argued about Simon we hadn't been getting on too well. I was really upset about that – and I think Jeff was too. So this trip was also our way of making up.

But Jeff was acting really strangely. He'd bought this baseball cap which he was wearing round the wrong way and he kept telling me how tough and hard he was.

I just wished he'd be his usual self. We had hardly any money so we decided we'd just buy a mask at *Jolly Jokes Galore*. This shop was right on the edge of town and always looked dark and dreary. The paint was peeling off its sign. And inside there was an old, musty smell. A man in a grey overcoat glared fiercely at us. He had a very long red nose which Jeff was certain was false; he was always daring me to pull it.

We started looking through the masks of grinning clowns and famous people. All the ones I remembered from last time were still here, only covered in an extra layer of dust. Did he ever sell anything? I wondered.

Then Jeff exclaimed, 'Look at that!' and held up a mask I'd never seen before. It was of a werewolf.

It looked really horrible. The fur which hung down from the top and sides of the mask seemed real. So did the blood dripping from its long yellow fangs. I hated it. Yet I couldn't stop looking at it.

Then all at once Jeff put it on. His grey eyes glinted at me from the werewolf mask.

'This is what I'm wearing tonight,' he cried. 'I dare you to get one too.'

I hesitated.

'Go on,' he said. 'This is much better than going as some boring old clown.'

'All right,' I said slowly. I thought there might be only one werewolf mask in the shop, but the shopkeeper climbed up his step-ladder and solemnly brought down another one. He wrapped mine up. Jeff wore his out of the shop.

'At the party tonight,' he said, 'I'm going to jump out at people and say, '"I want your blood".'

'Vampires say that . . . not werewolves,' I corrected.

'I know,' said Jeff at once. 'What do were-wolves say then?'

'They don't say anything, just growl a lot and attack people . . . and they howl, don't they?'

Immediately Jeff started practising his howl. He kept his mask on all the way home.

I didn't try my mask on again until I was getting ready to go out. I dressed all in black and I found these woolly gloves with long

fingers – I suppose they looked a little like claws. Then I caught sight of myself in the mirror. I'm not one of those very pretty, sweet-looking girls like Rat-bag Sarah. My hair's my best feature – it's dark brown and quite long; it goes down past my shoulders now.

But otherwise I'm just normal, I suppose, except for my skin. It's deathly pale. Some-one said once I looked like a ghost. I do try and brighten myself up, like recently I wore this really glittery dress to a party, Jeff immediately shouted out that I looked like an astronaut. I suppose an astronaut is better than a ghost.

Tonight, though, my skin seemed paler than ever. Sometimes I just hate the way

I look. Then I put on the werewolf mask. I looked a bit peculiar but not at all scary until I switched off the light.

At first the darkness seemed to swallow me up. I couldn't see anything at all. But then I started to make out the outline of a face. And suddenly I wasn't me any more. I was turning into someone else. I was turning into a monster. I gave a low howl. It sounded muffled, and surprisingly deep, nothing like my voice.

I shuddered.

Wouldn't it be awful if I couldn't change back – if I was doomed to wear this mask for the rest of my life. No-one would ever see me again. They'd always be running away from me. I gave another longer shudder.

Was the mask growing tighter?

It felt tighter.

I ran forward and switched on the light. At once I was just a girl in a mask from the joke shop again.

Then Jeff turned up. My dad was giving Jeff, Simon and me, of course, a lift to Rat-bag Sarah's party. At first Jeff and I were going to call round Simon's house in our masks. But then we thought it might be scarier if we hid in the back of the car and jumped out at him.

So Jeff and I hid underneath the back seat while Dad gave Simon a 'we're ready' toot on the car horn.

We crouched down in the darkness. I could feel Jeff's breath on my face. Then the car door opened. 'Hello, everyone,' said Simon.

'Well, hello Simon,' said Dad. 'I'm not sure where Jeff and Kelly have gone to,' he added. My dad always likes to join in our jokes.

Simon peered round enquiringly, and that was our cue to spring up, roaring and howling. And Simon just froze. He didn't laugh at us or pretend to be scared. He just stared and stared as if he couldn't believe his eyes.

'What do you think you're doing?' he said finally. His voice was shaking.

'We're being werewolves, of course,' replied Jeff indignantly.

Without another word Simon turned round to the front.

'What's wrong, Simon?' I asked.

He just shook his head. He didn't speak to us all the way to the party. Jeff kept whispering to me, 'You know what's wrong with him, don't you? He's jealous because our costumes are better than his.'

I found that hard to believe. Anyway, Simon's costume – tracksuit, boxing gloves and towel round his shoulders – was fine.

But something was certainly wrong.

We arrived to find the party in full swing. There was Batman, Superman and Superwoman, several pirates and pop stars and Sarah, as a ballerina! She pirouetted over to me. 'You and Simon have had a quarrel, haven't you?'

'No, why?'

'Oh, I just wondered,' she replied, before

pirouetting off again. She'd obviously noticed that Simon never came near Jeff and me all evening.

Jeff was having a great time, though, rushing round the party and jumping out at people. He seemed braver behind that mask. And when someone called him 'The Barrel', he gave this really loud, bloodthirsty howl, which made everyone at the party look round.

That was when Simon walked out of the party. I thought he'd just gone outside to get some fresh air or something. I went after him. But he'd gone. Later someone told me they'd seen him running up the road.

I told Jeff. He said, 'Oh, let him go, no reason to spoil our fun.'

But the party was ruined for me. Shortly afterwards I rang up my dad to pick us up.

When I arrived home I saw Simon. He was sitting on the wall in his front garden. He looked so sad I almost went over to him. But then I remembered I was angry with him for just running off like that without a word to me or Jeff. So I ignored him and quickly walked inside.

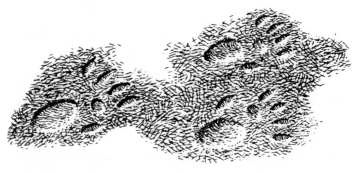

That night I woke up with a start. I always keep my window open at night. And although it has caused me major moth problems in the past (I used to hate it when moths would drop out of the air and on to my hair and once on to my mouth, but actually,

they've got quite interesting faces up close),
I love to fall asleep listening to that shim-
mering noise the wind makes rushing
through the trees or the faraway whistle of
a train. Or the new sound of dogs barking
and yelping next door. Those noises relax
me. It's only silence which keeps me awake.

But tonight there was a new noise.

One of the dogs was howling – and it was
the saddest sound I'd ever heard. I wondered
if it was Plute, the dog which had been badly
treated before Simon's family adopted it.
Was that dog remembering some cruelty
now? The howling just went on and on.

I wanted to run next door and put my arms
around poor Plute. But then I heard what
sounded like Simon's parents outside and
the howling stopped.

I hoped someone was patting Plute now.

Early next morning my dad said to me,
'Simon's at the door.'

I saw him waiting nervously for me in the
doorway, hands clasped behind his back.
'Hello,' he said.

'Hello,' I said coldly.

'I'm sorry I ran off last night.'

'You didn't even say you were leaving. It was just so . . . rude.'

'I know.'

'So why did you do it?'

'I was upset,' he whispered.

'About what?' I demanded, but my tone was a little gentler now.

He stared at me as if he didn't know what to say then he stared down at the ground. He looked so awkward I couldn't help feeling a twinge of sympathy for him.

'Jeff reckoned you were jealous of our costumes,' I prompted.

'Yes, that was it,' he replied at once.

'But your costume was all right.'

'Not as good as yours though, and the fact you both had the same mask made me feel out of it, I suppose.'

I shook my head. 'That's so silly.' But I couldn't help smiling too.

'Anyway, these are for you,' he said, and from behind his back he produced a large box of chocolates with a large red ribbon on the box, and they still had the price on them as well, £4.50.

I'd never had a present from a boy before.

I felt all shivery. I hoped my face wasn't turning red. 'You shouldn't . . . but they're lovely,' I croaked. 'You'll have to help me eat them,' I added.

'I think that could be arranged,' he grinned. 'See you later.'

Then I called after him, 'Oh, by the way, was it Plute I heard howling last night?'

Simon looked startled.

'I heard a dog howling last night, so I thought . . .'

'Oh yes, that was Plute all right. Sorry he woke you up.'

'No, don't worry about that . . . it's just that he sounded so sad.'

'He's happier now,' replied Simon. 'Much happier.' And his green eyes shone so brightly they seem to cast their own light.

That afternoon Simon returned; between us we polished off the entire box of chocolates. I felt a bit sick afterwards – but very happy too.

Buying me those chocolates was such a sweet thing to do. Simon obviously had a heart of gold.

I decided to keep the empty packet, so I put it in the top drawer of my dressing-table with my other special presents and cards, but they were all from my mum and dad and other relations, like my nan. Somehow, this was even more special.

I never thought I'd throw it away. But I did, just two weeks later.

CHAPTER THREE

One week after Sarah's party I got the biggest shock of my life.

It was Friday afternoon and it was only Simon and me coming home from school that day, as Jeff was away with a bad cold.

We'd just turned into our road when Simon's mum came rushing up to us. 'You haven't seen Plute anywhere, have you?' she asked.

'No, why, what's happened?' demanded Simon.

'I just opened the door for a second,' said Mrs Doyle, 'and Plute shot straight past me.'

She shook her head and sighed. 'Look, I'm going to drive around. I'm sure I'll see him. Will you wait at the house, Simon, and keep an eye on the dogs?'

Then she rushed off again. Simon looked worried. 'Poor old Plute,' he said. 'He's all mixed up.'

'I'm sure your mum will find Plute,' I said. 'I'd stay and wait but . . .'

'Yeah, I know, you've got to visit your nan.' He smiled. 'Have a good time.'

'I won't. I'll see you tomorrow – and Plute.'

'That's right,' he said, but he still looked anxious.

At home Mum and Dad were waiting for me. 'At last,' cried Dad. 'Well, get changed as quick as you can. We told your nan we'd be there for five o'clock and you know how she worries if we're late.'

My nan is totally ancient. This is quite handy when you're doing history projects on the War of the Roses or something, as she loves reminiscing – especially about her time in Cornwall. She'd lived there for years.

But after Grandad died, Nan moved near

us. She now lives in this little cottage with a huge garden, and whenever you visit her you have to walk around it – admire all her plants and vegetables.

Still, I quite enjoy visiting Nan – even though she hasn't got a television, just a crackly old radio which has always got discussions on it about how to get moss off your grass.

But today I wanted to stay at home and wait for Plute, only I knew my parents would never let me do that. So I reluctantly put on my 'going to see ancient relatives' clothes. Mum asked me to fetch her scarf. I went into my parents' bedroom and glanced idly out of the window, noticing it was starting to rain. Then I saw something which made me forget all about my mum's scarf: Plute.

45

He was running right in the middle of the road, chasing after every car which passed him. But he could get killed doing that. I sped downstairs.

'Where are you going, Kelly?' demanded my dad.

'Got to get Plute.' And before he could reply I ran like crazy up the road.

'Plute, here Plute, come on boy,' I called. A car swerved to avoid Plute; the owner yelled out of the window at me, 'That dog should be on a lead.'

'I know,' I yelled back. 'Sorry.'

Then for a moment, the road was clear. I raced over to Plute. 'Good boy, come on then, Plute,' I murmured, while half-dragging him on to the pathway. He wagged his tail cautiously at me. Then a car passed and Plute let out a low growl. I gave him a hug. 'What were you doing running in the road like that?' I whispered. 'Still, you were coming home, weren't you?'

As if in agreement, Plute wagged his tail more enthusiastically. 'Come on then, Plute, let's take you back and out of this rain.' For it was raining quite hard now. And with one

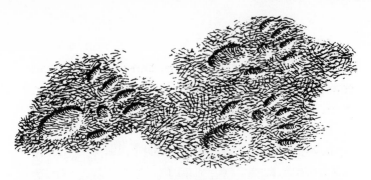

hand still on his collar I led him down the road. Plute clearly recognized his house because as soon as we drew near he yelped excitedly.

'Yes, that's your home all right,' I said, 'and Simon's going to be so pleased to see you back.'

To my surprise the front door was ajar so I let Plute rush ahead of me. He obviously knew exactly where Simon was. The kitchen door was one of those swing doors, so Plute could nudge it open. Chart music burst out of the kitchen followed by Simon's voice exclaiming, 'Plute, where have you been? Look at you, you're all wet.' The door swung half-shut and Simon's voice grew more muffled. I guessed he was bending down and whispering to Plute just as I'd seen him do before.

I should have left then. Plute was back

home – and my parents would be going mad wondering where I was.

How I wish I'd left then.

But I didn't. I wanted Simon to know it was me who'd brought Plute back.

The kitchen door was pushed open again. 'Now, stop it, you're still wet,' said Simon.

But Plute obviously didn't want to be dried. I could see the bottom half of his body wriggling about.

'Simon . . .' The word stopped in my mouth. As I'd seen something.

Then I saw it again, moving across Plute's back.

It was a hand. But a hand covered in hair. Thick, black, bristly hair. And the finger-nails were very sharp and pointed – like claws.

I'd only ever seen a hand like this once before. It was in the window of *Jolly Jokes Galore*. It was called *The Monster's Claw*. I remember Jeff saying to me, 'If that claw was real, it could rip your ear off with one swipe.'

And I'd shivered when Jeff had said that even though I'd known it wasn't real. There was something about it which made me uneasy.

But this claw . . . what was it?

WHAT WAS IT?

'Where did you find Plute, Mum?' Simon's voice. I couldn't reply. I couldn't move.

Simon pushed the kitchen door open a little further. 'Mum,' he began. Then he gazed up at me. And at once all the colour fell from his face.

Plute bolted away with the towel sliding off his back while Simon slowly got to his feet. I let out a thin cry when I saw him, saw both his terrible claws.

The monster's claws.

I started to back away from him.

'Kelly, wait!' he shouted. For a second I glimpsed an ashen face staring into mine.

But then my eyes returned to those hideous claws.

'I've got to go,' I croaked, looking behind me for the door which was suddenly a thousand miles away.

'All right, run away then,' he cried suddenly. 'I don't blame you. Who wouldn't run from these?' He raised both his hands in front of him. 'Who wouldn't be scared?'

'I'm not scared,' I gasped. 'I've just got to go home. Truly I have.'

'Oh, Kelly,' he said, 'you really weren't meant to see this.' He shook his head sadly, then walked back inside the kitchen, closing the door behind him.

This was my chance to escape from the monster. I should have sprinted out of there right away. But Simon wasn't a monster. He was my friend: someone whom I liked very much. He would never harm me, would he?

I was all confused.

'I thought you'd gone,' said Simon, standing in the kitchen doorway. He was watching me with a curious expression on his face.

'No . . . no,' I spluttered. Then I started edging towards the front door again.

He raised his hands; they were hidden in his black gloves again now. 'No-one's ever supposed to see what lies behind these gloves.'

'Well, don't worry about me. I hardly saw a thing really.'

'I'm only supposed to take these gloves off at night, but my hands get so hot and sticky and they itch, too . . . So how did you get in here?' he demanded suddenly.

'The door was open so . . .'

He gave a groan. 'I must have been so worried about Plute I forgot to shut it . . . You brought Plute back, didn't you?'

'Yes, he was running in the road. I saw him.' My voice kept trembling.

'I wish you'd stop looking at me like that.'

'Like what?'

'Like I'm about to eat you up.'

I laughed shakily. 'Don't be silly.'

'Well, come a bit nearer then.'

I moved forward about one millimetre. Plute appeared again; he stood beside Simon panting excitedly. Simon bent down and patted him, then whispered, 'It's because of you Kelly knows my terrible secret. You've given me away, Plute.' Then he looked up at me. 'The doctors told me in a couple of years my hands will be back to normal. So I've just got two more years of this.' He gave this really unhappy laugh. 'I'm counting the days off on my calendar, I really am. I hate being a freak.'

'You're not a freak, Simon,' I said softly.

His large, green eyes stared intently at me. Then he whispered to Plute, 'I told you she was my friend, didn't I?' Still gazing down at Plute, he whispered, 'Can I ask you a big favour?'

'What's that?' I replied, my voice nearly as low as Simon's.

'Don't tell anyone what you saw today. Will you promise me that one thing? Please.'

Before I could reply the doorbell sounded, making me jump. And then I heard my mum call, 'Sorry to barge in but . . . Kelly, what are you thinking of? You're supposed to be round your nan's. You can see Simon tomorrow. Oh, Simon, I know your mum and I only exchanged keys for emergencies, but the plumber still hasn't called. If he turns up would you ask your mum to let him in, only . . .' My mum rattled on while I stood there in a daze.

I spent the next few hours like that.

'You're very quiet,' said my nan to me that evening. 'And you've hardly eaten anything.' She felt my forehead, then announced to my mum, 'Yes, the child is definitely sickening for something.'

'Well, her friend Jeff is away from school and I thought Simon looked a bit peaky this afternoon; there's obviously something going round. How do you feel, dear?'

'I do feel a bit groggy,' I said. This wasn't a lie – although I knew I wasn't ill.

On the way home my parents put a thick blanket around me. I sat in the back of the car thinking, thinking, thinking. If only I'd seen scabs or scars or hundreds of spots on Simon's hands – they were the sort of nasty things anyone could get.

But I'd never seen hands as hairy as Simon's. It was almost as if he'd had an animal's hands grafted on to his body.

I shivered.

But he said it was all caused by some medical ailment. Why couldn't I believe him?

I did believe him. I just wanted more proof. Maybe my parents would know. 'Mum, is there a medical condition which makes your hands go all hairy?'

'Hey, watch out, I've got hairy hands,' said Dad.

'No, I don't mean like that. I mean masses and masses of hair.'

Mum turned and smiled. 'I think you've been reading too many spooky stories.'

Dad added, 'If you ever see anyone with hands like that, Kelly, run for your life.' Then he and Mum roared with laughter.

I stared miserably outside at the dark, rainy night and the cars swishing past. The windscreen wipers whirled backwards and forwards and they seemed to be saying: run for your life. Over and over they repeated it: *Run for your life. Run for your life. Run for your life.*

Next day was Saturday. My parents fussed over me, saying how pale and drawn I looked. In the afternoon, just to get away from them, I said I wanted to go for a walk.

They finally decided a bit of fresh air might do me good. 'Why don't you call for Simon?' said my mum.

'Yes, yes,' I murmured. I didn't know whether to or not. It was already getting dark outside. I hate it when the days get swallowed up so quickly.

I walked past Simon's house. He was sitting at a table in front of the window, writing. A pale yellow lamp was on beside him. It made the whole room look warm and welcoming. Then he looked up and saw me. He immediately signalled that I should come in.

Why shouldn't I go in? Simon was my friend.

I followed him through to the room where he had been writing.

'You're not doing homework, are you?' I said.

'No, I'm writing to Lawrence, a good mate of mine.'

I nodded, interested. Simon hardly ever spoke about his friends. 'Did he used to go to your old school?'

'Yes, that's right,' said Simon vaguely.

'So where was your old school?'

'Cornwall,' he muttered.

'Oh, really, my nan used to live there, back in the Dark Ages.'

Simon grinned and changed the subject. Then his mum came in, made the fire up for us and insisted I had some hot chocolate as I 'looked perished'.

We sat on the couch in front of the fire. We chatted about school and how much Simon liked playing for the school football team. I tried to relax but I felt nervous and awkward somehow. I think Simon did as well. For he suddenly whispered, 'You didn't tell anyone about . . . yesterday?'

'No,' I replied firmly.

'I knew you'd keep your promise,' he said warmly. 'If anyone had to find out I'm glad it was you.'

I blushed at the compliment. 'Did you tell your parents?' I asked.

A look of horror crossed his face. 'Oh no, they'd go mad – especially my mum. She'd hit the roof.'

I shivered without quite knowing why. His mum reappeared with a tray of hot chocolate and biscuits.

'Make sure you drink it all now, won't you, Kelly?' she said.

Why was she so keen on me having this hot chocolate? Because Simon did tell her what I'd seen and now she wants to poison me? At once I knew I was being totally silly.

But even so, I sipped the hot chocolate very slowly. The dogs raced around us begging for food, and we talked about other things. But I couldn't get what I'd seen out of my mind.

'About yesterday,' I said. 'There was just one thing I wanted to ask you.'

'Keep your voice down,' whispered Simon.

Then with a trace of irritation, 'What is it, then?'

'I just wanted to know the proper name of your illness.' For then I thought to myself I could look it up.

'What an odd question,' said Simon, looking suddenly quite fierce. 'What does it matter anyway.'

'Oh, it doesn't,' I said quickly.

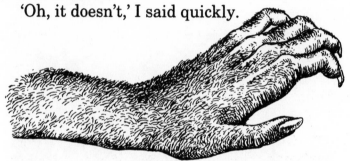

'OK, my hands are different to yours. I've got this — well I wouldn't even call it an illness — but anyway, it's not infectious. You'll never get it, so what does it matter what it's called. I'm the same person I was before you found out.' His voice rose. 'I'm still me.'

The door opened. His mum looked in. 'Everything all right?'

'Fine, thanks, Mum.'

'Good, good,' she murmured, looking all around the room. Nice as his mum was, I felt as if she was checking up on us – or me.

I wondered again if Simon had told her about yesterday. There was something going on in this house, wasn't there? Something I didn't know about. Then Dad's words started echoing around in my head: *Run for your life. Run for your life.*

I sprang to my feet. 'I've got to go,' I announced.

'What, already?' exclaimed Simon.

'Yeah, I told my parents I'd only be ten minutes, so I'm already in trouble . . . I'll let you get back to your letter.'

'OK then, well, come round anytime.'

'Thanks.' I fled before his mum could appear again.

That night I really wanted to tell my parents everything, but I couldn't. That would be like sneaking on Simon. Besides, I'd promised.

Then I suddenly remembered I'd never actually promised Simon anything. The doorbell had gone before I could say anything. Still, Simon thought I'd promised him. And that was the same thing.

Or was it?

CHAPTER FOUR

On Monday morning I walked to school with
Simon. We chatted about the new number
one in the charts (we both hated it), a thriller
which had started on television last night,
and oh, so many things. It was a perfectly
ordinary conversation. So why did I feel we
were both acting?

Jeff was still away from school. I missed
him. I'd meant to go and visit him last night.
But then I figured Jeff would realize something was worrying me right away – he's
pretty quick like that – and before I knew it

I'd be blurting out Simon's secret. And I really didn't want to do that.

If only – if only Simon would tell me the name of the illness which had turned his hands into . . . claws.

That's all I needed to know. And if Simon really was my friend he'd tell me, trust me.

I decided to have one last go. 'Simon, can I ask you something?'

He turned sharply as if sensing what I was going to ask. And he looked so hurt as if I was about to let him down.

I swallowed hard. 'So when are you playing for the school football team again?'

Immediately the atmosphere relaxed. And then we met two of the boys from the football team. They really liked Simon. Everyone did – except Jeff. But would they be patting Simon on the back now and laughing and joking with him if they knew his secret? Would they even be talking to him?

Simon gave me one of his big smiles. 'See you later, Kelly,' he said. He was acting as if everything was just the same.

But it wasn't.

To be honest, I was glad when Simon went

off with his mates. I needed time to think. I walked into school, and down the long corridor to my form-room.

'Hello, Kelly,' called a voice.

'Hello,' I replied absently, lost in thought. Then I realized who it was. It was the school nurse. I looked up, amazed at how she seemed to remember everyone's name.

And then I had an idea.

The school nurse could tell me if Simon was lying or not. I wouldn't mention him by name, of course. I'd just ask her casually if there was an illness which turned your hands all hairy. That wouldn't do any harm, would it?

I went over to her: 'Excuse me . . . can I ask you something, please?' My voice was shaking all over the place.

'Yes, of course, Kelly, come in.'

She was a large woman with a very red face and false teeth which moved up and down every time she spoke. I went inside her room. There was nowhere to sit except for this couch in the corner. And I didn't want to lie down as if I were ill or something. But then she found me a chair.

I felt nervous. 'What it is,' I began, then all in a rush, 'This sounds a bit of a silly question, but is there an illness which makes your hands turn hairy, I mean, really hairy – and your nails go all pointed and sharp too?' I paused for breath.

The nurse just opened her mouth wide. She didn't say anything, while her teeth wobbled uncertainly. Then she made this sucking noise – I think she was rearranging her teeth – and asked sharply, 'Is this some kind of joke?'

'Oh no,' I cried.

She sucked her teeth again thoughtfully for a moment. Then in a gentler tone, 'You know, Kelly, there was a boy at my school who claimed his hands had turned purple. He got us girls proper scared. It turned out it was just the dye from his gloves but it looked most realistic. I must say he had me fooled. I'm assuming it's a boy this time too.'

I nodded.

'Boys don't change, do they? He's pulling your leg, love. You tell him, if he's got hands like that Nurse wants to see them, he's a medical marvel.' She got up. 'You cut along to your lesson now. I think we've wasted enough time on your friend, don't you?'

Part of me wanted to tell Nurse that I'd seen those hands with my own eyes, but I couldn't do that. Still, at least I knew for certain Simon had been lying to me.

An angry tear crept down my face. I quickly brushed it away. And then I saw Simon. He was leaning against the wall opposite the school nurse's room. What was he doing there? Was he following me?

'Someone said they'd seen you go in the

nurse's room. Are you all right?'

'I'm all right,' I muttered. I wasn't going to tell him anything so I just walked away from him, brushing away another angry tear. Then I turned round. He was still staring after me. A cold shudder crept up my back. I practically ran to my form-room.

That night I went round to Jeff's house. Jeff's mum was standing outside talking to their next-door-neighbour, Mr Prentice, an oldish man with a very large, egg-shaped head and no neck, so he looked as if he were permanently shrugging his shoulders. He spent most of his time now staring out of the window. He even ate his meals looking out of that window. He used to be a big-game hunter, or so he claimed. Certainly his house was full of stuffed animals which I thought was creepy and horrible.

'Ah, come to visit the young invalid, have we?' he said.

I hate it when people talk to me in that patronizing way. So I just answered, 'That's right,' and stared at Jeff's mum.

'Go straight up, dear,' she said. 'I'm sure Jeff will be very pleased to see you.'

But when I opened Jeff's bedroom door he called out very sarcastically, 'Oh, how nice of you to come round. I thought you'd forgotten who I was.'

'Don't be silly,' I replied. 'You know I had to go to my nan's on Friday.'

'And Saturday, and Sunday.'

'I was busy then too.'

'Well, I'm glad someone was enjoying themselves.' His voice was hoarse and his nose was bright red.

'Are you still feeling bad?'

'Terrible.' He blew his nose vigorously as if to prove it. 'Why do I get more colds than anyone I know? My sisters never get colds' – Jeff had two sisters, both older than him –

'and they're always out somewhere. It's not fair.'

'I brought you these. I wasn't sure if you already had them.' I handed Jeff two super-hero comics.

He glanced at them. 'I have got them, actually. I must have every superheroes comic in the world, but thanks, anyway. Sit down – and get rid of her, will you?' He nodded at a woman who was babbling away on his little black-and-white television set.

I switched her off and sat down on the edge of Jeff's bed.

'So, got any hot news for me?' he demanded. 'I've been bored out of my skull up here.'

'Well, actually I have . . . it's about Simon.'

Immediately Jeff sank down in his bed again. 'Don't tell me, he played for the school team on Saturday morning and scored eighty-seven goals with his eyes shut.'

'No, nothing like that,' I said.

Jeff looked at me. A light came into his eyes. 'What's up, Kelly?' he asked.

'It's a secret, actually. It's . . .' I stopped. I felt as if I was about to betray Simon. But

Simon had lied to me, so my promise to him didn't hold any more. It wasn't even a real promise anyway. 'If I tell you this secret, do you promise not to tell anyone else?'

'Yes, all right, just get on with it.'

Then I told Jeff everything. And it was such a relief. At last someone else knew. When I'd finished Jeff shook his head. 'This is a wind-up, isn't it?'

'No, it's not a wind-up,' I replied firmly.

Jeff let out a low whistle of amazement and said, 'Well then, he's a werewolf.'

At that we both burst out laughing. Finally, I said lightly, 'How could he be a werewolf?'

'He's hairy enough to be one,' said Jeff. 'Imagine shaking hands with him.'

'Oh, don't be horrible.'

Jeff grinned. 'Do you suppose, in the morning his mum goes, "Now Simon, have you brushed your hair and your hands?"'

I giggled. 'And when he goes to the hair-dresser's, do you think he gets his hands cut too?'

'Probably has them shampooed,' said Jeff. We started laughing again at the absurdity of it all.

'I've just thought of something,' said Jeff. 'Do you remember when we wore those were-wolf masks and he got the hump about it – well, maybe he thought we were on to him.'

'No . . .' I began.

'Well, it could be. After all, your bedroom does look out on to their back garden. And no-one else could see past all their trees and stuff. Only you.'

I gulped, then said slowly, 'You won't tell anyone, will you, Jeff? You promised.'

'All right,' he muttered. 'But I reckon I should keep a log of all this, just in case . . .'

'In case of what?'

'Well, with those claws he could rip your head off without blinking,' said Jeff.

'Oh, thanks,' I cried.

Jeff leaned forward eagerly. 'And if a werewolf sinks its teeth into you, you become one too. And I saw this film recently where they scratched someone and that's pretty bad too. You . . .'

'All right, all right,' I interrupted. 'Look, aren't we forgetting something here? We're talking about Simon. Our friend.'

'Well, he's more your friend than mine.'

'Who's got this medical condition . . .'

'Which no-one has ever heard of.' Then, seeing my face, 'OK, Simon might just be seriously weird. But there's no harm in being careful, is there? That's why I'm going to write down everything that's happened and then put on the front: "This is strictly private. Only to be read in emergencies, like getting your head ripped off." That's a joke,' he added quickly. 'By the way, are you going to tell Simon I know?'

'Er . . . well . . .'

'Only it's probably best I'm undercover.' Jeff picked up a notebook. 'Now, I want to get every detail written down.'

Later that evening, when I was back home, Jeff rang me. 'I'm speaking on my dad's mobile,' he said proudly. 'Have you got anything to report?'

'Not yet.'

'I've written it all up now, seven and a half pages . . . I also wanted to tell you to keep your bedroom window closed tonight.'

'Why?'

'It's best not to take any risks with a werewolf about.'

'So what do you think it's going to do, leap into my room in the middle of the night?'

Straightaway I wished I hadn't said that, especially when Jeff replied, 'Werewolves can jump very high, you know, and . . .'

'Jeff, goodnight,' I replied, slamming the

phone down. What had started as a joke – making out Simon was a werewolf – wasn't funny any more. I had a feeling Jeff had started to believe it.

Just because someone's got hairy hands and long fingernails doesn't mean they're a werewolf, does it? I felt ashamed of myself for telling Jeff now.

That night I fell asleep almost at once, but then I woke up with a start. I knew there was something in my bedroom. I'd heard it move.

I froze with horror.

Once before I'd heard something at night. And then I'd seen it waddling along the carpet. The shock made me scream. My dad came racing to my room and then we both tried to catch it – a bird that had flown in through my window.

'Don't hurt it,' I cried as my dad lunged for it. But it kept fluttering away. My dad said it was like trying to get hold of a bar of soap. We were ages. Finally I caught the bird. I remember, it had tiny pink legs. Then with a flurry of feathers the bird soared out of my hands and into the cold night. Had another bird flown in tonight?

My eyes were getting used to the dark now. I sat up and peered cautiously around my room. Then I stared down at the carpet. Something stared back at me.

The most hideous face I'd ever seen.
This time I was too scared even to scream.
I knew I mustn't move. I must keep as still

as possible. But I couldn't stop my heart thumping. It was deafening. I'd seen something so horrible and nasty . . . and all at once I knew what it was. I stared down at that face again – its jaws open wide, showing all its cruel teeth.

It was my werewolf mask.

It must have fallen off the back of the door. And the noise of its falling must have woken me. Funny how it's often the tiniest little sounds which wake you up, isn't it?

I knew, though, that I couldn't sleep with that hideous face lying on my carpet. I had to tuck it away in the cupboard. But first, I wanted the light on. I climbed out of bed. I knew the mask wasn't real but I still crept gingerly round it, just in case it suddenly moved.

My bedroom's quite small but tonight my journey to the light switch seemed to take a million years. My hand reached for the switch then something brushed against my legs. I gazed down in terror to see Muffin staring up at me.

'Oh, Muffin, don't do that,' I gasped. I switched on the light. But the room still wasn't bright enough. I sat on the edge of my bed with Muffin beside me. I stroked her head. 'You shouldn't have sneaked in like that, but I'm really pleased to see you. You can be my bodyguard tonight.'

I bent down and picked up the tip of the werewolf mask and then flung it into the back of my cupboard. Tomorrow, I thought to myself, I would chuck it out.

I was just climbing back into bed when this howling noise started. Muffin immediately stiffened and started hissing.

'Don't be afraid,' I whispered. 'It's only Plute – a sad, lonely dog.'

Yet Plute sounded different tonight: louder and fiercer, like a wild beast declaring its supremacy. I shivered. Then I became angry with myself. Plute wasn't a wolf. He was a tame labrador with a weakness for chasing cars. Wolves don't exist — not in Britain anyway.

And werewolves don't exist anywhere. I looked around for Muffin. She'd gone. 'Muffin,' I whispered. Then I spotted my 'bodyguard' crouching underneath my bed. I tried coaxing her out. But Muffin wouldn't budge.

Meanwhile that howling noise grew louder. Now it seemed to fill my room. What was it?

It was a werewolf.

What nonsense.

But I suddenly sprang up and closed my window tightly. Now the noise was much fainter. I took a deep breath. Then I saw Muffin emerge from her hiding place. I picked her up and put her on to the bed.

I sat stroking her for a while. Usually after a few minutes Muffin will jump down and go on her way. But tonight she stretched herself right out on to my legs. I think she was still scared.

She wasn't the only one.

CHAPTER FIVE

Next morning Muffin had gone. And my room felt very stuffy. So I got up and opened the window a little. I heard the whirr of the milk-float and the crates rattling. Those noises reassured me.

I decided I'd over-reacted last night. Just because I'd heard a dog howling I'd started imagining things. It was pretty silly really. Still, the first thing I did after I got up was hurl that werewolf mask in the bin.

Dad was on holiday this week, so over breakfast he was boasting about all the decorating he was going to do. 'You won't

81

recognize the bathroom when I've finished,' he said.

'We'll believe that when we see it, won't we, Kelly?' said Mum, winking at me.

'I wouldn't be surprised if Dad is still sitting here when I get back from school,' I replied.

It was fun teasing Dad. It made last night seem far away. Then the telephone rang. It was Jeff.

'Any news?' he asked breathlessly.

'Well . . . I heard this howling noise . . .'

'That's him, Simon the werewolf,' cried Jeff. 'I hardly got a wink of sleep last night you know, thinking about it all – and finding out things. Did you know that tonight is a full moon?'

That news took me by surprise. 'No, I didn't.'

'I also wanted to warn you,' whispered Jeff urgently.

'Warn me?'

'Well, if Simon is a werewolf – he'll want to make sure you keep his secret, won't he?'

'I suppose so,' I said cautiously.

'So he might do something to prove his

power and say, "Don't mess with me."'

'Like what?' I said in a small gasp.

'I think he'll kill – well, he might kill Muffin, for a start.'

'What?' I cried, and immediately started looking for Muffin.

His voice rose. 'I'm not saying it will be Muffin definitely. I just think he will do something.'

The doorbell rang.

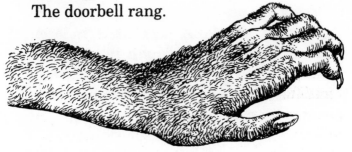

'Answer that, will you, Kelly?' called Mum.

'Is that him?' asked Jeff.

'I expect so,' I replied. 'Anyway, thanks very much for ringing. You've really cheered me up.'

'I'm only trying to help.' Jeff was indignant. 'I've been up all night thinking about this.'

'Well, anyway, look on the bright side. If Simon really is a werewolf, at least we know what to get him for his birthday: a razor.' I sniggered at my little joke. But Jeff didn't.

'Just be careful, Kelly, won't you?'

He sounded so scared I felt scared too – for about a second. But then I laughed to myself. Jeff was talking rubbish – as usual. I opened the door. And then I saw . . .

I knew at once it was dead. It was a bird. A thrush, I think. A poor little innocent thrush. Simon was holding it in his gloved hand. But he was waving the dead bird in the air as if he was proud of what he'd done, as if it were some kind of trophy.

Simon was also saying something to me. But I couldn't listen to him. I was too upset, too horrified by his crime. 'How could you have killed that bird?' I screamed at him. 'How could you?' I screamed so loudly my mum and dad rushed out of the kitchen.

'Whatever's happened?' began my mum. Then she saw Simon standing there with the bird in his hand and immediately declared, 'Oh no, not again. That's the third time this month Muffin has done that. I'm always telling her off about it.'

'I'm afraid it's a cat's nature,' said my dad, sadly. 'Did you find it on the step, Simon?'

He nodded gravely. 'It looked so awful just lying on the step. I thought it would be best to bury it.' Simon spoke quite calmly but his hand was shaking.

'I think Muffin leaves them there as a kind of present,' said Mum. 'It's a thrush, and they're so tame as well.' Then she turned to me. 'In the past you've always been at school. I know it is upsetting to see.' Mum gave my hand a squeeze. 'Why don't we bury the thrush by the bushes over there?'

I stood in the doorway and watched while

Mum, Dad and Simon dug a little hole for the bird. It had been horrible seeing that poor, dead bird. But something else upset me too. It was my thinking Simon had killed it. I felt so ashamed.

Dad insisted on driving us to school as he thought I 'still looked a bit shaky'. Simon and I sat in the back. We didn't say one word to each other. Dad obviously thought I was still in shock and rattled on about 'nature's chain'.

'Keep an eye on her, Simon,' said Dad when we reached the school gates.

As soon as Dad had gone Simon said, in a horrible, choked kind of voice, 'You really thought I'd killed that bird, didn't you?'

I was so full of shame and embarrassment I could hardly look at him. 'No, Simon . . . no, I didn't. It's just, well, I didn't sleep very well last night and the way you were holding it made me . . .'

'Oh, come on, at least be honest,' cut in Simon, harshly.

In a flash I retorted, 'Like you've been honest with me, like you've told me the truth about your hands. No-one's heard about that illness you mentioned.'

'What do you mean?' gasped Simon. 'You haven't told anyone my secret?'

'No, well not exactly. I mean, I didn't mention you by name.' That, of course, was a lie. I became confused and embarrassed again. I looked up at him almost pleadingly. 'It's just that what you told me . . . it doesn't make any sense,' I began. But then I saw his huge, green eyes. They were alight with fury. I couldn't help noticing something else; his face seemed much hairier this morning. He had the beginnings of a small moustache now and there was hair growing on his neck too.

I stepped back.

'You'd better not have told anyone,' he said, his voice low and menacing.

'Why, what are you going to do?' I taunted,

but I sounded much braver that I felt. Before he could reply a group of boys came up. 'Three–one,' they chanted. 'Spurs was annihilated on Saturday.'

'No, we played well. We just didn't get the chances,' replied Simon. He went off, laughing and arguing with them. Only this time he didn't say 'See you later' or smile at me.

He didn't even turn round . . .

Why should he? We weren't friends any more.

I certainly didn't want to walk home with him after school. But as it happened, during break, Simon ran out of the form-room saying he had a really bad headache.

Later I heard his mum had taken him home.

When I arrived home Mum said, 'There's someone waiting to see you,' and I jerked in horror, thinking it was Simon. But, instead, it was Jeff.

'I'm feeling a bit better so your mum's invited me round for tea . . . not that I've quite got my appetite back,' he added, piteously. 'But I think I could manage something.' In fact, Jeff managed two platefuls of fish fingers, chips and baked beans and a large helping of fruit trifle. Afterwards we escaped to my room where I gave Jeff a full report of what had happened during the day.

When I'd finished Jeff looked at me for a moment, then said significantly, 'I don't think Simon went home because he had a headache . . . it was because he was turning into a complete and total werewolf. I mean, you said he looked a bit hairier first thing this morning, didn't you?'

'Yes, that's true.'

'Well, he could probably sense more hair was about to sprout up so he had to get out of school fast. By now I bet his face and body will be totally covered in hair.'

I started to picture this while Jeff went on, 'He'll have hair everywhere now. In fact, he probably won't be able to see very well, he'll have so much fur hanging over his eyes. You wouldn't recognize him tonight, Kelly.' Then his voice became graver. 'But you're in danger, especially now he knows you haven't kept his secret. Simon probably suspects you've told me. So I'm in danger as well. When I go home tonight he could be waiting to jump out at me or something.' He gave a nervous laugh. 'We'll have to tell someone, like your parents – or mine.'

I got up. My head was in a whirl. 'I don't know,' I began.

'We've got to.'

'But what can I tell them?'

Jeff gave an impatient gesture. 'How

about that your next-door-neighbour has got claws for hands and is at the moment turning into a full-scale werewolf?'

'No,' I said, firmly, 'that would be really sly.'

'Sly,' echoed Jeff contemptuously.

'Yes, I mean we don't know for certain Simon is a werewolf.'

'How much more evidence do you need?' cried Jeff.

'You want him to be a werewolf, don't you?'

'And you still really like him, don't you?' replied Jeff.

We stood staring accusingly at each other until I suddenly laughed. 'Do you remember when you thought there was a monster at the bottom of the garden?'

'Oh, that was millions of light years ago.'

'You even went and told your mum there was a monster there. And she just said, "Oh, that's nice, dear."'

'Well I think that's charming bringing that up,' said Jeff. But he couldn't help laughing too.

'So maybe, Jeff, when you tell your mum

about that werewolf she'll just go, "Oh, that's nice, dear."'

Jeff seemed to smile and frown at the same time. 'The trouble is, adults never check things out. I mean, they won't go and pull Simon's gloves off and see for themselves. What we need is more evidence.'

Out of his sports bag (although Jeff hates sports), he produced the log-book – 'We must write everything down in here' – and a pair of binoculars. 'They're not brilliant but they might help us keep watch. You don't mind if I stay over, do you, Kelly?'

'Of course not. I'd be really happy if you did actually.'

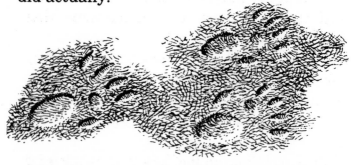

Jeff grinned at me. 'Werewolves have to be outside during a full moon so I'm sure we'll see something tonight.' Then he got up. He was so excited he couldn't stand still. He was practically dancing around my room.

But then our plan hit a snag. Jeff's mum wouldn't let him stay over. In fact she wouldn't let him stay past seven o'clock. She said he still hadn't built his strength up and needed a good night's rest.

So despite all his pleading, Jeff had to go. I was on my own.

I lay in bed wondering what I was going to see tonight. Maybe nothing? Maybe Simon really was ill and was fast asleep now?

Maybe.

I heard my parents trudge up the stairs. And Muffin made a brief appearance. She didn't stay tonight though.

I parted the curtains a little bit. A grey mist looked in on me. I could hardly see anything or hear anything either – just the occasional yelp from one of the dogs next door.

My eyes began to feel heavy. I decided I'd just rest my eyes for a moment. I climbed back into bed and immediately fell asleep.

I felt guilty when I woke up; Jeff would be

93

very disappointed with me. I should get out of bed and watch again. But I was also very sleepy and my bed was warm and soft.

It was then I heard it.

A howling noise.

I tumbled out of bed and over to the window again. But I couldn't see a thing. The mist had swallowed everything up. Simon's garden had vanished. Even the howling had stopped as suddenly as it had begun. But I couldn't lose the feeling that something was out there crouching in the darkness.

And then out of the mist sailed what looked like a large white bubble. It cast an eerie paleness over everything. Now I could see . . . I could see there was someone in that garden.

CHAPTER SIX

I couldn't see the figure in the garden very clearly. But I knew it was Simon. He was standing very still underneath a tree in the middle of the garden.

My hand shaking, I reached for the binoculars. It was hard to hold them steady and the moon was already slipping away again.

Just for a moment I saw Simon's face, half-lit by the moonlight, half in darkness. But I saw enough.

I saw that hair had grown right across Simon's eyebrows and his chin. I saw there

95

was hair covering his ears and he had what looked like massive sideburns too. Only all the hair seemed to hang off Simon's face as if it didn't quite fit him.

My skin went cold. He looked hideous. He was a freak, a monster. There were no other words to describe him.

Then he tilted his head upwards towards my room. Had he seen me? I let go of the curtains. The binoculars jumped out of my hands. My legs wobbled. I fell on top of my bed.

Had he seen me? The question tore around my head. I felt he could still see me.

For ages I was too scared to move. I just sat there. My window was still open. But all I could hear was the blood pumping in my head.

Finally I got up and drew back the

curtains a centimetre. And then another centimetre. The moon was hidden once more. All I could see now was the mist pressing against the window.

It was almost as if I'd dreamt what I'd seen. But I knew I hadn't. And I knew I'd never forget what I saw, not if I lived to be a hundred and forty.

I felt sick – not with fear but with disappointment. Jeff was right: Simon really was a werewolf. Simon had lied to me. He'd probably only pretended to be my friend to keep me quiet.

Of course his family were in on it as well. I remember now how they had cross-examined me about my bedroom and whether I was a light sleeper. Maybe they were werewolves too: a whole nest of werewolves living next door to me. Goosebumps ran up my arms.

I pictured the three of them sitting round the table tonight . . . all heavily bearded. That was such a weird image I started to laugh softly.

Then I thought of Simon again, and his pretending to be my friend.

I got up and rustled through my special drawer I brought out the wrapper from the box of chocolates he had given me. And I tore it up into tiny pieces. Then I got into bed again and wrote down everything I'd seen tonight in Jeff's log-book. In giant capitals at the end, I wrote:

NOW I KNOW FOR CERTAIN
SIMON IS A WEREWOLF

CHAPTER SEVEN

In the dark the phone rang loudly and urgently. I squinted at my watch; it was exactly seven o'clock in the morning. No-one ever rings at that time unless it's something very serious.

But what? Maybe . . . maybe Simon's told his parents that I know he's a werewolf? So now they're ringing to tell my parents they'd better keep me quiet or else?

I crept to the top of the stairs. Normally when my dad answers the phone his voice booms around the house. But today I could hardly hear him. Then he put the phone down and started whispering to Mum.

'Who was that on the phone?' I called. I wanted to know – and yet in a way I didn't.

There was some more whispering and then Mum came upstairs. She sat on my bed with me. 'That was Nan's next-door-neighbour. Your nan had gone outside to feed the birds first thing in the morning as usual, when she had a fall.'

'Is she all right?'

'Yes,' replied Mum firmly. 'But your dad and I will be going down to see her and we might bring Nan back for a few days.'

I nodded gravely.

Usually I just have cereal for breakfast but today Dad made some hot buttered toast and the three of us sat around the kitchen table talking about Nan. Mum and Dad kept saying how strong Nan was, and telling funny stories about her.

'Don't you worry now, Kelly,' said Dad. And I suddenly realized they were both staring at me.

'You do look pale this morning,' said Mum.

'I always look pale,' I muttered. 'Ghosts envy me my complexion, you know.'

Mum ignored this. 'There's nothing else worrying you, is there, dear?' she persisted.

Only that I know for certain our next-door-neighbour is a werewolf, that's all. I longed to tell my parents the whole story. For the secret was now like a giant heavy weight dragging me down. But I knew this wasn't the right moment. I decided I would definitely tell my parents tonight: whether Nan was here or not.

Mum and Dad were outside packing the car when I heard Mum say, 'Oh, I'm sorry to hear Simon isn't very well.' I went outside to discover Mum talking to Mrs Doyle, with the two West Highlands bounding around their feet.

'Well, I do hope Simon's better soon,' went on Mum, giving me a 'I'm surprised you didn't tell me' look.

I quickly scrutinized Mrs Doyle's face for any sign of a beard. To my disappointment I couldn't see any.

'Hello, Kelly,' she said to me. But her smile wasn't as friendly as usual. 'I was just telling your mum about Simon not being well.'

'I heard,' I snapped. I wasn't going to pretend with her. We both knew the real reason why Simon wasn't going to school. Then feeling suddenly daring, I said, 'Could I see him for a moment please?'

Mrs Doyle's eyes wobbled. 'I'm sorry, Kelly, but he's asleep.'

'Are you sure?' I replied. Mum gave a little protesting cry at my rudeness. But I didn't care. Soon my mum would discover our neighbours' terrible secret.

'He's fast asleep,' replied Simon's mum firmly. 'But I'll tell him you called.'

'Yes, do that, won't you,' I replied, then walked off.

'Take care, Kelly,' Mrs Doyle called after me. I didn't like the way she'd said 'take care'. Was that another threat?

In the house Mum came up to me. 'Is everything all right between you and Simon?' she asked.

'No, Mum, it isn't,' I mumbled. 'But it's a long story, so I'll tell you about it tonight.'

Before Mum could reply Dad bounded in. Jeff had called. He was going back to school today. And Dad said he would give us both a lift.

In the car Jeff and I talked in a kind of code. 'How's Simon?' he asked.

'He's still not himself,' I replied. Then I said, 'Here's the notes you missed, Jeff,' and handed him the notebook. Jeff read avidly what I'd written down last night. He couldn't say anything. He just looked at me and mouthed, 'Wow!'

As we walked into school Jeff said, 'This is a really amazing discovery. You know, this could make us quite famous . . . if we live to tell the tale.'

There wasn't time to talk any more. School was freezing that day and lots of pupils were complaining. In the end we were allowed to keep our coats on during lessons. Then, just before lunch, there was an emergency assembly. The whole school jostled into the sports hall where, to loud cheers, the deputy headmistress announced that the heating had broken down and so everyone – apart from Year Eleven – had to go home. Then, to equally loud groans, she announced that school should be back to normal tomorrow. Still, a half-day's holiday was not to be sneezed at.

Jeff and I raced out of school and back to my house to work out a plan of action. 'The big problem,' said Jeff, 'is still getting anyone to believe us.'

We went up to my bedroom. I glanced idly out of my window, never suspecting . . . I spotted Simon out of the corner of my eye first. He was sitting cross-legged on the grass with all four dogs gambolling around him. The hair around his face looked even thicker that it had last night. And it was more shocking seeing him in the daylight somehow. It was like having a nightmare in the middle of the afternoon. I was about to alert Jeff. But there was no need.

'Look!' cried Jeff in a strange, hoarse voice. His eyes kept darting between me and what was outside the window. 'Look!' he repeated. Then he suddenly gripped my arm tightly and started pulling me away from the window. 'Got to be careful,' he stuttered. 'Werewolves have got hyper-hearing. Maybe he can hear us now.' Then he went and sped down the stairs and into the kitchen. I was right behind him.

Without a word Jeff filled up a glass of water. His hand shook as he gulped the water down. Then he turned to me. His eyes had gone all glassy. 'Never thought I'd see that . . . not in real life,' he whispered.

'Jeff, come and sit down.' He looked as if he was about to pass out.

Jeff fell on to a chair.

'And I'm sure he can't hear us otherwise he wouldn't be in his garden, would he?' I said.

Jeff looked up. 'That's true . . . he thinks we're still at school . . . and where do you reckon his parents are?'

'Well, I know his dad leaves for work very early and his mum helps out at the dog sanctuary part-time. She's always going on about it – and how important it is . . . what?'

For Jeff had suddenly stood up. 'I've just had a brilliant idea . . . why don't we take a picture of the werewolf?'

'What, from my bedroom window?'

'No, it's a bit far away. We could climb up the fence.'

'Climb?' I exclaimed.

'Or . . . or one of us could sit on the other's shoulders, quickly snap a picture and that's all the evidence we need. They'll have to believe us then.'

We gazed at each other excitedly. It sounded almost too easy.

'There's just one small problem,' I said. 'I haven't got a camera.'

'You must have.'

'I'm sorry, I haven't. My dad has one somewhere but I'm pretty sure it hasn't got a film in it as . . .'

'We've got a camera,' interrupted Jeff, 'and it's a polaroid so you have your pictures right away. I'll go and get it?'

'Yeah, but be quick, won't you. He could go back inside at any minute.'

Jeff wiped his forehead. 'All right, don't keep on . . . all this stress. I still can't believe it. Him just sitting in the garden in his jeans and T-shirt. Him – a werewolf.'

'Jeff,' I cried urgently.

'OK, don't worry, I'll run my fastest.'

I tried to look impressed. But Jeff always came last in cross-country.

I watched him wobbling and wheezing down the road. Then I darted upstairs to check the werewolf was still in the garden. He was – but for how much longer?

Hurry up, Jeff.

Finally he came panting into view with a large camera round his neck. I opened the door and Jeff practically fell inside. His breath came in hurried gasps. He managed to say, 'Sorry I'm late . . . it was my mum . . . wanted to know why I wanted the camera.'

'What did you tell her?'

Jeff turned bright red. 'I told her I wanted to take a picture of you . . . it was all I could think of.'

'So when you go home with a picture of a werewolf . . .'

'She'll say, "Oh what a nice picture of Kelly. She's much more attractive than she used to be."' We grinned at each other for a moment. 'Is he still outside?' asked Jeff.

'He was the last time I looked.'

Jeff handed me the camera. 'There's only two pictures left by the way.'

'So I'm taking the picture, am I?'

Jeff shrugged. 'Well I thought it would be best as you're the lightest.' He paused.

'Yes, OK.' I took the camera. 'So what do I press, this button here?'

'Yeah, that's right. It's dead easy.' Then he added, 'When we're in your garden we mustn't talk. We must move like shadows.'

We didn't say a word until we reached the fence. 'Ready,' whispered Jeff. I swallowed hard, and nodded. He knelt down. I took my shoes off.

I climbed on to his shoulders. As he straightened up again, he hissed, 'You're much heavier than you look.'

'Sssh.'

'And did you know your feet smell?'

'They do not,' I hissed back indignantly. 'And stop shaking about.'

'Just hurry up, will you? I can't hold you for much longer.'

Now I could see over the fence. Simon was curled up on the grass. His eyes were closed. One of the West Highlands had snuggled down against his knees, while Plute was lying next to Simon's head.

'Come on,' whispered Jeff.

I aimed the camera. I wanted to get as much of Simon's face in as possible, and those werewolf hands too.

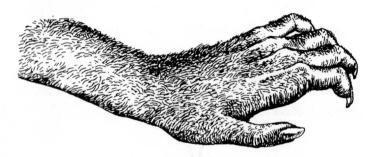

Plute's ears pricked up. He saw me. He gave a low growl. Simon muttered something to him. He sounded half-asleep. But I knew I had to take the picture now.

I pressed the switch just as Simon suddenly bolted upright. There was a great flash of light. Simon's eyes popped wide open as if I'd just shot him. He gave a great howl of pain. Then he fled into his house with the dogs barking beside him.

All at once I felt myself wobbling. Then I tumbled on to the grass.

'Sorry,' said Jeff apologetically. 'But I couldn't hold you a second longer . . . Still, you got it, didn't you?' Jeff pulled the photo out of the camera.

He waved it about in the air. 'This helps it develop . . . but I think we should look at it inside.'

Scrambling into my shoes, I followed Jeff into the kitchen where we peered at the picture. Nothing seemed to be happening to it.

'I've just thought . . . maybe you can't take pictures of werewolves because they're dead,' said Jeff.

111

'It's vampires who are dead, not were-wolves,' I replied snappily. 'Werewolves are . . . well, they're not dead anyway.' Then I cried, 'Look, something's happening.'

'Hey, I can see him,' said Jeff excitedly.

It was Simon's eyebrows which came out first, so bushy they seemed to have been joined together. Then those great clumps of hair which looked so weird hanging off an eleven-year-old's face.

'I wonder what it's like growing that enormous beard overnight. Hey, will you look at his eyes. He looks as if he's about to attack someone . . . probably you, and that camera.'

'I think he was just very shocked,' I said.

'And you've got one of his paws in too . . . that's not a bad picture at all, Kelly. I mean, you might have got a bit closer but actually we have all the evidence we need now. We've done it.'

We looked at each other.

'So now we can tell people,' went on Jeff.

'We are doing the right thing, telling people, I mean?' I asked.

'Kelly, he's a werewolf,' cried Jeff. 'What

about if he attacks someone? We'd feel really guilty then.'

I agreed with him, but I still had this horrible, sick feeling in the pit of my stomach.

'Shall I tell my mum then?' asked Jeff.

'Yeah, your mum will know what to do.' I closed my eyes for a moment. I felt dizzy. 'It's up to her now.'

'Are you sure you'll be all right here?'

'Oh yes.' I looked at my watch. 'Besides, my parents will be home soon.'

'And you will be careful about opening the door, won't you?' said Jeff anxiously.

I nodded. Then I asked, suddenly, 'What do you think will happen to Simon?'

'I don't know, maybe he'll be put in a zoo.'

'Locked up, you mean?'

'Well, you couldn't have tigers roaming the streets, could you? And he's much worse,' said Jeff. He got up. 'Remember, don't answer the door until you're certain who it is . . . If it's me I'll ring on the doorbell four times at once.' He gazed down at the photograph. 'Even now,' he said, 'I still can't believe it . . . a real-life werewolf living next door to you.'

After he'd gone I closed my eyes again. I felt strangely drowsy and drifted off to sleep. I dreamt I visited Simon at the zoo. It felt really bad until he escaped and started chasing me. The doorbell made me leap to my feet. It only rang once, so it couldn't be

Jeff. I stumbled to the door. 'Who is it?' I cried, as bravely as I could.

There was a pause, then, 'It's me, Simon. Let me in.'

'No, no. Go away.'

'Come on, Kelly, let me in . . . it's dangerous for me to be on your doorstep like this.'

'Dangerous for who?' My voice came out in a kind of croak. 'I've got nothing to say to you . . . just go.'

Then there was silence. Had he gone? I stood waiting, but I couldn't hear anything else. My knees were still shaking. I sat down, then almost at once I shot to my feet. What was that banging noise? It seemed to be coming from the garden. I rushed to the window in the dining room just as Simon leapt over the fence and into my back garden.

CHAPTER EIGHT

Simon was in my garden.

I felt scared and helpless. If he could leap over fences what else could he do?

I stared out of the window at him. He came closer. Then his face was right up against the glass.

I thought I was going to scream. But I didn't. I just stood there whimpering with fear, like some terrified puppy.

'Let me in, Kelly.'

It was so odd hearing Simon's voice coming out of a face which was not Simon's at all. It was as if he was wearing a terrible mask. And any second now he'd peel it off, and there would be Simon back again. But this wasn't any mask. He really was a . . .

'Get away, you werewolf, get away!' I cried.

At once he stepped back from the glass. Then he let out the loudest, most terrible howl I'd ever heard. It seemed to make the whole house shake. I started to shake too.

'Just go away!' I screamed. I sprang forward and started drawing the curtains. Then I rushed around the rest of the house frantically drawing the other curtains too.

There was silence. Had the werewolf

jumped back to its own garden? Or was it still hiding out there somewhere, just waiting for me to venture outside and then . . .?

He only needs to scratch you and you'd be a werewolf too. Wasn't that what Jeff had said? So I didn't dare go anywhere. I was trapped in this dark, shadowy house.

Oh, where was Jeff?

Why weren't he and his mum round here now? I ran to the phone and dialled Jeff's number. Let him be at home. Please let him be at home.

There was no reply.

Perhaps he and his mum were on their way round here?

But I had to talk to someone now. My mum and dad. How I wished I'd told them before. Nan's number was there by the phone. So I rang it.

There was no reply.

That must mean my parents were on their way home. But how much longer would they be? I didn't think I could stand another moment here alone.

Then the doorbell rang – three times.

Could that be Jeff? It'd be just like him to forget the code is four times not three.

It must be Jeff.

I raced to the front door. 'Who is it?'

No answer. Then the letter-box was pushed open. 'Kelly, open the door, please,' called a voice. It was Simon's mum. She scared me nearly as much as Simon.

'Just go away!' I screamed. 'My parents will be back any minute,' I added.

'We must talk first,' said Simon's mum, firmly. 'Come on, open the door at once.' Her tone was pleading yet I sensed she was angry with me too.

'No,' I began, then I stopped. I remembered something which made my blood turn to ice: Simon's mum had got a key. She and my mum exchanged keys, didn't they.

Then I heard a key turn in the lock.

CHAPTER NINE

The front door opened. I wanted to rush upstairs and hide in my bedroom. I nearly did. But then I thought, this is my house so why should I run away. Instead, I stood by the stairs gripping the bannisters tightly.

Simon's mum was standing in the hallway trying to smile reassuringly at me.

'Get out of my house now!' I cried.

'Yes, I will go, and I haven't closed the front door so you're perfectly safe,' she replied. 'But first you must let me explain . . .'

'Why?' I interrupted rudely. 'So you can tell me some more lies?'

'Kelly, whatever you think I just beg one thing of you – that picture you took, please don't show it to anyone. At least promise me that.' She sounded really scared. This made me feel a little braver.

'Answer me this first,' I said. 'Simon is a werewolf, isn't he?'

She took a sharp intake of breath, then whispered, 'Werewolf is such an ugly, melodramatic word. We never use it. But yes . . . my son is a wolf-boy.'

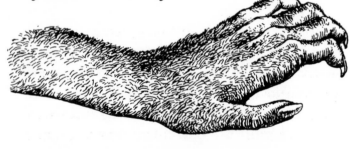

I began to feel afraid again. 'How long has he been one?'

'You're born a wolf-boy, Kelly. There's no other way. All those lurid stories in the cinema about people being bitten by wolves and turning into wolf-men is just nonsense

. . . dangerous nonsense. It causes such pain to us when, in fact, being a wolf-man is a calling, something to be proud of: the most wonderful gift. Simon's great-grandfather on my side was a wolf-man, so we hoped Simon might . . .'

'You hoped?' I said, disbelievingly. 'But look what happens to him . . .'

'Is his face so terrible?' she asked.

The question embarrassed me. I wasn't sure how to answer her.

'No-one's allowed to be different, are they?' went on Mrs Doyle.

'I didn't say that.'

'I think you did. You know, Kelly, when I was about thirteen I found my face was covered in spots. Those spots lasted for about two years and I felt so self-conscious about them. I'd see people turning away from me in the town. Even friends didn't seem to want to be my friends any more. Everyone changed, except me. I was the same person I'd been before . . . Simon's never had a spot in his life. But for about two or three years certain full moons cause hair to form all over his face and body – for a

couple of days. By tomorrow most of that hair will have disappeared. And by the time he's sixteen the hair on his hands will all have gone too. He may still have to shave two or three times a day, rather than once, when there's a full moon . . .'

'But otherwise he'll be normal,' I interrupted.

'Well, often wolf-men remain superior athletes – and it's not just during a full moon they can run faster, and jump higher than any man – and their hearing and sense of smell remains as sharp as any dog's. But they always use their superior powers to help mankind. Always,' she repeated, 'but then wolf-men are braver and more loyal than any mere man could be.'

The front door suddenly swung open.

Simon stood in the doorway.

'What are you doing out of the house

124

again?' exclaimed his mum. 'You, you know how dangerous it is for you.'

'I'm all right,' he said quietly. Then he looked across at me. 'Mum has told you the truth, hasn't she?'

I nodded.

'I'm glad,' he said. 'I wanted Mum to tell you.'

'It was Simon's idea I come round,' said his mum.

'I knew you wouldn't listen to me. I knew you were scared of me.' There was more than a hint of bitterness in Simon's voice. I couldn't look at him. I just kept staring at the carpet. I felt all twisted up inside.

'I warned Simon not to go in the garden on any account. But he so loves to be outside at this time and as you were all away he thought it was completely safe. I told him there's never a time during the day when it's completely safe, didn't I, Simon?'

'Yes, Mum,' said Simon absently. I knew he was staring at me. But I still couldn't look at him. Then Simon walked slowly towards me. When he was standing right in front of me he unclenched his right paw; I saw there a medal attached to a dark blue ribbon. 'I wanted to show you this . . . you can look at it if you like.'

I shivered slightly as my hand touched the hair on Simon's hand. But then I stared down at the medal. It was gold, although a bit tarnished. On one side was the profile of a king and on the other was what looked like an angel with arms outstretched. Around the edges of the medal was printed: AWARDED TO SIMON GARSON FOR BRAVERY OCTOBER 1919.

'My great-grandad,' said Simon. He spoke very quietly but there was no mistaking the pride in his voice.

'Simon's great-grandad helped track down some of the country's most dangerous criminals,' went on Simon's mum. 'Without him, many more people might have lost their lives.'

I kept on staring at the medal. To be honest, I didn't know what to say. 'Thanks for letting me see this,' I said finally. I handed the medal back to Simon. 'Do you want to be a detective like your great-grandad?' I asked.

'No, I want to help find people. At the moment I only have special powers – special animal powers – during a full moon. But later they'll be mine all the time. Then I'll just have to smell something and be able to track someone from hundreds of miles away. So I want to find people who go missing. I'd really love to do that.' He sounded so eager and enthusiastic, so like the Simon I'd first met that I suddenly looked up at him and into those dark, green eyes. And it was there I found Simon again. He'd been there all the time, of course. But it was only now I could see him again.

'I'm so sorry,' I cried.

'What for?'

'For not trusting you.'

'I don't blame you,' he began. 'It was only when you thought I'd killed that bird . . . you really upset me then . . . I wanted to tell you the truth from the start, you know.'

'But I wouldn't let him,' said Mrs Doyle. 'That was my one condition when we moved here. You see, Simon had never been to school before.'

'Never!' I exclaimed.

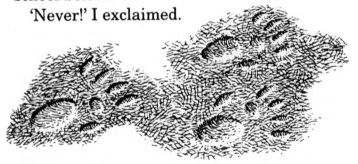

His mum smiled faintly. 'Simon has spent all his life at a special home for wolf-boys, far away from prying eyes. His father and I would visit him – and stay over at weekends. But Simon was so eager to go out into the world and go to a real school . . .'

'I read every school story there ever was,' he interrupted. 'I was just desperate.'

I said, 'That first day when you called for

me I thought you seemed a bit over-eager.'
We both grinned at the memory.

'When his father got a new job near here
we saw this house to let and, more to the
point, so did Simon. He begged and begged
us for his chance. We wanted to, of course,
but we also knew how very, very dangerous
it was.' She lowered her voice. 'If the world
found out about Simon's powers some
unscrupulous men could try and use him for
their own evil purposes . . .' She shook her
head. 'Sometimes men can be much more
dangerous than any dog – or wolf.' She
paused. 'And then there are other people
who would want to lock Simon away because
he was different . . . that is why, Kelly, I do
beg you not to show that photograph to
anyone.'

'But of course,' I began, then, with a jolt of
horror I remembered I didn't have the
picture: Jeff did. Goodness knows how many
people he'd have shown the photograph to by
now.

What could I do?

'Kelly, are you all right? You look a bit
groggy,' said Simon. His voice was gentle

and concerned. 'Do you want to sit down?'

'Yes, yes,' I said. Maybe I could think better sitting down. So many thoughts were whirling around in my head.

So I sat on the couch while Simon and his mum sat opposite me. Then Simon asked, 'Do you mind if I sit on the carpet? I find it more comfortable – at the moment.' He sat cross-legged on the carpet, then looked up at me. 'Go on then, ask me anything.'

'Anything at all?'

'Yes. I want to tell you everything now,' he cried.

I considered. There were so many things I wanted to ask him. 'That howling at night; it was you, wasn't it?'

He nodded. 'That huge kennel you saw, that's like my other bedroom. I'm always out there during a full moon. I do try to be considerate but howling at night, it's such a natural thing for me . . . like singing or whistling or playing the drums – only much, much better, especially during a full moon.'

'What does a full moon feel like then?'

'Well, even if it's the middle of winter you wake up thinking it's a boiling hot summer's

day, you just cannot get cool . . . that's the first sign. Often that's the only one. But then you have the odd full moon which really gets you: then you start to burn up. That's what happened to me at school yesterday. I've never been as hairy as this before,' he added apologetically. 'I've even got hair all down my back this time. Still, it does have its brilliant side too. I mean, your sense of smell is so strong you can smell everything, you can even . . . you can even smell the seasons changing. That's why I spend all night in the kennel during a full moon. It's so intoxicating out there, Kelly.'

'I can imagine,' I replied. And I could. I

was picturing it all. And I was so happy until a swift, dark cloud came over me blocking out everything . . . THE PHOTOGRAPH. I had to warn him. But the words didn't want to leave my throat.

'I'm sorry, we must stop there, we have to go,' said Mrs Doyle. 'It isn't safe for Simon to be out of the house today.'

'But can't I just stay a few more minutes?' said Simon. 'It gets so lonely shut away on my own.'

'No, Simon, I'm sorry,' replied Mrs Doyle firmly. Then she added more gently, 'Maybe Kelly could come and see us later. Maybe. Now I shall just check it's all clear outside . . . when I come back be ready to leave at once, Simon.'

'Mum,' Simon called after her. But she had already gone. He shrugged his shoulders. 'I just wanted to tell her – it's too late.'

'Too late?' I echoed.

'Listen,' he said.

Then I heard it – and saw it too. My parents' car pulling into the drive. 'Oh no, what are we going to do?' I cried.

'I don't know,' said Simon lightly. He didn't look scared at all.

'You must hide,' I said.

'Oh yes, I must hide,' he said slowly. 'But don't worry, I know all about hiding.

Outside a car door slammed shut. I saw my mum. Then I saw my nan struggling out of the car. I began to panic now. What would Nan do if she saw Simon – fall down in a dead faint?

'Simon, you'd better hide in my room,' I said.

'Sure, OK,' he said, but he didn't exactly rush up the stairs, and he gave me this sad grin as if to say, 'This is all so silly, isn't it?'

The doorbell rang. I sprang forward. Mum was helping Nan up the four steps to our door. 'As you can see, Kelly, your nan's come to stay for a few days.'

'Hello, Kelly,' said Nan, extending a hand

as tiny as a doll's to me. She was a dwarfish figure with wispy hair that was still a beautiful auburn colour and eyes as bright as a bird's. As usual, she was wearing a hat; this one had on it the longest feather I'd ever seen.

'All this fuss. I just slipped on the step, that's all,' muttered Nan. 'Could have happened to anyone.'

'Now you come and sit down,' said Mum, helping Nan over to the sofa. 'You've drawn the curtains a bit early, haven't you, Kelly? Draw them back, will you, dear.'

In a kind of daze I drifted to the window. Light poured into the room again. My mum was chattering on. 'Now I'd better go and pick your father up from the supermarket. He should have got everything by now. Then we'll unpack your bags, Nan. Now, will you be all right?'

'Of course I will,' replied Nan brusquely.

'Kelly will make you a nice cup of tea – and if you'd like to go up to your room Kelly will help you, won't you, dear?'

I nodded. My mum drove away. I smiled at Nan. 'Would you like a cup of tea?'

'No thank you.'

Then the phone rang. I hoped and hoped it was Jeff. It was Mrs Doyle.

'Kelly, you must get Simon out of the house.'

'Yes I know. I'll do my best,' I whispered.

'I'll be waiting outside,' she said.

'OK, I'll be as quick as I can. Bye.'

'What's going on? Who are you whispering to?' demanded Nan.

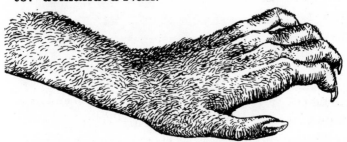

'Oh, just a friend,' I croaked. 'Are you sure you don't want a cup of tea?' Nan didn't answer. But she kept staring at me. Dare I try and get Simon out now?

And then from upstairs came the unmistakeable sound of a sneeze.

I stood there for a moment, horror-stricken. But Nan didn't appear to have heard anything. I started to breathe again.

Until Nan announced suddenly, 'I think I'd like to go upstairs. Will you help, Kelly?'

'Of course, Nan,' I said. Nan leant on me, although she wasn't heavy at all. We slowly walked up the stairs. My mind was racing. Once Nan was safely in her room, that would be the ideal moment for Simon to creep downstairs.

I helped Nan into the guest-room. She said she didn't want to sit down just yet. But she'd love a glass of water. I sped off to get her one, while Nan immediately started nosing around. For of course she'd heard that sneeze. And now she was doing some investigating of her own. She didn't have to look very far.

I rushed back upstairs. Then I nearly dropped the glass of water with shock. I could hear Nan's voice. And Simon's. Trembling, I opened my bedroom door. Nan immediately turned round and beamed at me. 'At last I've seen one. I've seen a wolf-boy,' she cried in a voice full of wonder, as if she'd just discovered a mermaid or a unicorn in my bedroom. She turned to Simon who was sitting on the carpet, grinning all over his face. 'I'm so glad I've been spared to see this day. When I was a little girl my parents would tell me stories about the wolf-men and all the crimes they solved and how we could all sleep safer in our beds because of them. I longed to see one but I never did. Sometimes, late at night I'd hear them though. And once I saw this light far away in the Cornish hills and my friends told me that's where the wolf-boys lived.'

'That's right,' said Simon. 'There's a special home for wolf-boys . . . that's where I lived, actually.'

'I wish I'd heard those stories about the wolf-men, Nan,' I said.

'Didn't your dad ever tell you them?' Nan shook her head. 'But then I should have told you them myself . . . It's such a shame when the old stories get lost,' she added, more to herself than us.

Feeling embarrassed and ashamed, I said, 'The thing is, Nan, I didn't know about wolf-men so I . . .' Then I started telling her what Jeff and I had done. When I mentioned the photograph Nan interrupted sharply, 'Where is it now?'

'It's safe with Kelly,' said Simon. Suddenly he was looking at me, his eyes shining out of the dark. And I thought, if I could wish for one thing in the world it would be for that picture. Then I'd hand it straight to Simon – or burn it, or do whatever he wanted. I wondered what Jeff had done with it. I must find him. Where was he?

Nan was already urging us towards the door. 'It seems so rude to push you away, wolf-boy, and there's so much I want to ask you. But it's best you spend tonight in your house away from prying eyes.'

'I know,' said Simon. 'But it's been really great to meet you.'

Nan gave a wizened chuckle. 'This has been such a wonderful surprise. I couldn't be more excited if Sherlock Holmes himself had

138

walked in here.' She waved us off from the top of the stairs. 'I'll be all right here . . . be careful now, wolf-boy.' Nan said the word 'wolf-boy' so reverently it was as if she were saying 'Your Majesty'.

'I'll just go and see if your mum's outside,' I said to Simon. It was then the doorbell rang. Four times. 'It's Jeff,' I gasped. I was so relieved. Now I could get the picture back from him. 'You'd better hide in the sitting-room, Simon.'

'Just think, I'll have hidden in every room in your house soon,' he replied, with a weary smile.

'Get rid of them,' hissed Nan from the top
of the stairs.

'It's all right, Nan. I know who it is,' I said.
I opened the door to see Jeff, his mum and
someone else who I dimly recognized as
Jeff's nosy neighbour, Mr Prentice. He was
carrying a net.

I stared at him in amazement.

'It's in there, isn't it?' he said. 'I know it is.'

'I don't know what you're talking about,' I
began. But then my attention was caught by
Simon's mum, hovering in the driveway. It
was at that moment Mr Prentice suddenly
shot past me.

'No, wait. You can't go in there,' I cried.
But I was too late. He was in there. He was
in the sitting-room. Then he leapt about a
metre into the air and started snorting

through his nose like a horse. 'Mr Prentice,' I cried. 'I can explain.'

'Walk out calmly,' he gasped. 'Don't want to alarm it. No need to run now.' Then he vanished faster than a magician's handkerchief.

Simon stared after him. He smiled into his beard. 'Well, he didn't stay long, did he? I hope it wasn't something I said.'

CHAPTER TEN

Simon and I started to laugh. We weren't really laughing at his joke. It's just when I'm nervous or scared I'll laugh at anything. And right then we were both very nervous and very scared.

I saw the net which Mr Prentice had dropped on to the carpet in terror. 'And he says he used to stalk big game,' I said. 'I don't think so.' Simon and I laughed again, until suddenly I realized that net was meant for Simon. Simon could be sprawling around inside there now.

Simon looked at that net and shuddered. While in the hallway there were raised voices, Mrs Doyle saying, 'If you'll just calm down and let me explain.'

'No, I'm sorry, I can't calm down,' replied Jeff's mum. 'I just want to know exactly what's going on.' She marched into the sitting-room, saw Simon, and gave a horrified gasp. 'Is this some kind of prank you're all playing on my son? If so, I think it's in pretty poor taste. You've scared poor Jeff half to death.'

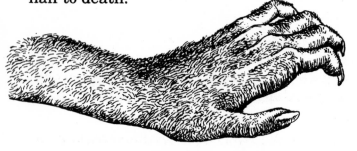

Jeff blushed deep red.

'Well, maybe your parents can explain what's going on,' went on Jeff's mum as a familiar car turned into our drive.

'They can't, but I can,' called a voice from the top of the stairs. 'Come on, help me down, Kelly.'

I helped Nan downstairs, just as my parents trooped inside. Dad was carrying a large box of shopping. He looked around in astonishment. 'We seem to have a full house.' He peered into the sitting-room, saw Simon and declared, 'Bit late for Halloween, isn't it?' Then he gave this apology of a laugh and froze. So did my mum.

Their faces seemed to be stuck in that horrified state until Nan said, 'I don't know why you're looking like that, son. I told you all about wolf-boys when you were little. Don't you remember?'

'Yes, I do,' said Dad. 'But I thought they were just stories.'

'Just stories,' said Nan in the same tone teachers use when you say the dog ate your homework.

'Well, no-one has ever told *me* any stories about wolf-boys,' said Jeff's mum. 'And I'm still waiting for an explanation.'

'I'll tell you all you need to know,' said Mrs Doyle. 'But only after you've put away that thing.' She nodded at the net. Dad hastily picked up the net and threw it in the back garden.

Then there was this great babble of voices as Nan and Mrs Doyle tried to explain while my parents and Jeff's mum kept interrupting. They seemed to be asking the same questions, over and over. Mrs Doyle was remarkably patient, I thought, but I noticed how her eyes kept darting out of the window. All the time she was watching, on the alert for danger.

Simon never said a word. He stood in the darkest corner of the room staring down at the carpet, as if he didn't want to hear what everyone was saying.

'Hello,' I whispered to him. 'How are you?'

'Dog-tired,' he replied, with a quick smile. 'I wish this was all over.'

I felt really sorry for him. I had to help him. But what could I do? There was one thing: give Simon the picture back.

I edged across to Jeff. 'They're giving me a headache,' moaned Jeff, nodding at his mum and my parents. 'Why are they asking so many questions? Are they going to write a fact-sheet on wolf-men or something? I understand it now. Why can't they?'

I nodded sympathetically, then asked,

'Can I have our photo back?'

He shook his head, regretfully. 'I'm afraid old man Prentice has got it.'

'Oh no. How could you give the photograph to Prentice?' I cried this out so loudly everyone turned around.

'What's this about the photograph?' demanded Mrs Doyle. 'I thought you had it, Kelly.'

'No,' I said miserably. 'I gave it to Jeff and he . . .'

'I gave it to Mr Prentice to look at,' interrupted Jeff's mum, 'as he knows about wild creatures and things . . . he examined the photograph through his magnifying glass for us to see if it was a fake. I mean, it could have been.'

'But we've got to get it back!' I exclaimed.

'Yes we have,' cried Mrs Doyle.

'I'm sure I shall be able to get the picture back from Mr Prentice without any problem at all,' said Jeff's mum. 'But not before I've had the answers to a few more questions from Mrs Doyle. There is the school, for instance. Now did they know . . .?'

'But there's no time for any of this,' I yelled. 'Really, there isn't.'

'Kelly, don't be so rude,' snapped my mum. She turned to Jeff's mum. 'I'm sorry, please finish what you were saying.'

'Thank you,' said Jeff's mum. She launched into her next question. But I noticed Simon was suddenly gazing all around him. He looked anxious. Then I saw why.

A large van was pulling up outside our house. Out of the van jumped two men in grey uniforms. They helped out of the van a third person: Mr Prentice. My heart started to thump. As all three walked quickly up our drive, I heard Mr Prentice saying, 'No, it lives next door but it was here earlier . . . of course, they may have evacuated the house.' Inside the sitting-room everyone had been startled into silence.

'If only you'd stayed inside, Simon, as you were told,' burst out Mrs Doyle, 'then none of this would have happened.'

'It's our fault, Kelly's and mine, not his,' said Jeff sadly. 'And yours,' he added, glaring at the adults, 'for just talking and talking all the time.'

The doorbell rang. 'I'll deal with this,' said Mrs Doyle, her voice strong again. My parents and Jeff's mum followed her to the door.

'You children stay here,' said Jeff's mum. She closed the sitting-room door but we could still hear . . .

'We're from the local authority, here is our I.D. We're concerned with exotic and dangerous creatures, and we're investigating a complaint that you are keeping a wild beast – without a licence – that is a threat to public safety. This is the picture we were given of it.'

'He must have the polaroid now,' hissed Jeff.

Then we heard Mrs Doyle say, 'That creature, I'm proud to say, is my son.'

'Good for you,' whispered Nan.

But the man went on, 'Do you have a licence for it, er, him?'

'Of course not,' said Mrs Doyle.

'And is he in the house now?'

'That's my business,' replied Mrs Doyle.

'We do need to see him,' the man persisted.

'It's the law,' said the other man.

'I've seen it, great terrifying thing it was,'

declared Mr Prentice, his voice carrying right down the road. 'And none of you are safe while this thing is roaming about.'

'Oh no,' I groaned. At the same moment Simon let out a low howl.

'Do you hear it?' shrieked Mr Prentice. 'Now do you believe me. I only escaped from it by the skin of my teeth. We're all in terrible danger.'

'Why won't he stop going on about it?' I hissed. 'He's getting everyone all wound up and . . .' I froze. I can't tell you how scary it is to look casually out of your window and see a face staring back at you. It was a man's face. He had cupped his hands and was peering intently at us.

'I think I can see something,' he called.

'Go away!' I screamed. 'Go away!'

'Or you're going to be really sorry,' added Jeff, after the man had gone.

'I don't believe that,' I exclaimed. 'The nerve of him, just barging up to our window like that.' The three of us looked at each other, shaken and incredulous.

'Now I know how animals in the zoo feel,' said Jeff, trying to make a joke of it. He and

I laughed uncertainly. 'We'd better draw the curtains over,' went on Jeff, 'just in case we get any more peeping toms.'

'No, it's all right, don't worry,' said Simon through clenched teeth. 'I've had enough. I'm going to sort this out.' Without another word he bolted past us.

'Simon, don't go out there,' I cried. Jeff and I rushed after him. But we were too late. Simon was already outside.

A large crowd was gathering. I recognized Rat-bag Sarah and her dad. There were cries of alarm when Simon appeared on the steps. Someone screamed and Sarah's dad jumped in front of her. Meanwhile the two men from the local authority looked as if they'd been hypnotized; they just stood there with their mouths open.

'Oh, Simon, why didn't you stay in the house?' cried Mrs Doyle.

'I'm just so tired of hiding, Mum,' replied Simon quietly. The crowd were backing further and further away. Most of them were huddling together in the middle of the road now. And they were eerily quiet, not saying a word. But their eyes were on stalks. They gawped and gawped at Simon until someone started to laugh. It was Sarah's dad. His laughter was loud and mocking.

'All right,' he said, 'it was a good joke. You had us all fooled, even me for a moment there. But you can take the mask off now.' That last sentence was more like a command.

Simon shook his head.

Sarah's dad came striding towards him. There were cries of alarm. But Sarah's dad just called out, 'We're all being played for fools. I'll show you what's going on. I'll bring that mask back with me.'

He was a large, paunchy man and he

towered over Simon. He wagged his finger reprovingly. 'You've had your fun but now I'm telling you again, lad, to take the mask off.' His voice was soft and confident.

Simon looked up at him with steady, green eyes. 'I promise you, it's not a mask,' he said.

'Of course it isn't,' added Mrs Doyle.

Sarah's dad leant forward as if he was going to whisper something in Simon's ear. Instead, he started pulling at Simon's beard. Immediately Mrs Doyle and me were yelling at him to stop. But Simon just stood there, not moving a muscle.

'What is going on here?' shouted Sarah's dad, tugging furiously at Simon's beard.

'You're hurting him,' I cried. 'Leave him alone.'

Sarah's dad finally stopped and staggered backwards. 'What is this?' he demanded angrily. 'We've a right to know.' But his voice had lost its pleased as punch smugness. And he was hissing fiercely, like a kettle about to boil.

'Answer him then,' called a voice from the crowd.

'Come on, speak,' cried someone else.

A ripple of wind ran through Simon's beard. And his head was tilted upwards slightly as if he were sniffing the air. I thought he looked magnificent. Then he raised his paw, at which there were more gasps. 'Please listen,' he said to the crowd. 'I may look strange to you – at first. But I come in peace.' He sounded as if he were a creature from another planet. Still, by the way everyone was staring at him, that was probably how he felt.

'I come in peace,' he repeated. 'And I can help you. I want to help you.'

'But you're a werewolf,' called a voice.

'Bolt all your doors tonight,' yelled Mr Prentice.

I shot him a look of utter contempt. But there were murmurs of agreement. 'Someone like you should be locked up,' said

155

a man, backing further away as he said it. There were even louder murmurs of agreement.

'No, look, please listen to me,' went on Simon. But his voice had sunk to a whisper. And then he just turned away. I don't think he could bear looking at that crowd any more.

I thought, Simon has risked everything tonight. He could have just hidden in my house. But instead, he'd gone out there facing everyone, because he wanted them to understand. If only they'd give him a chance.

They must give him a chance.

I burst out, 'You say he should be locked

up. But why? Because he looks different to you and me. Some of us know Simon, and like him a lot.' I looked straight at Sarah. 'Now tonight he's got some hair on his face and his hands, but look closer, it's still Simon, our friend. So please listen to him. He really can help us and . . .'

'The fact is,' interrupted Sarah's dad – something of his oily, confident himself again, 'I cannot allow someone like this, someone who's only half-human, to go to school with my daughter. Anything could happen.'

Sarah stared up at him. 'Dad, shut up, will you,' she hissed.

I shot Sarah a grateful look, but her dad wouldn't be silenced. He carried on yelling as if a gale were raging round him. 'I'm sorry, we really can't allow a creature like this – however reasonable he might pretend to be – to roam around freely, can we?' Everyone in the crowd – apart from Sarah – seemed to agree with him.

Then one of the men from the local authority whispered to Mrs Doyle, 'I think it's best if we talk inside your house. We do need to ask a few questions.' He sounded quite apologetic about it.

'Yes, all right,' said Mrs Doyle. 'Come on, Simon, let's get this over with.'

'We'll come with you,' said my mum. 'You go and keep Nan company, Kelly.'

I turned to Simon, who still had his head averted from the crowd. 'Simon, I'm so sorry. I really never meant this to happen. You must believe that.'

Simon gave me this big, warm smile. 'See you soon,' he said. He sounded really bright and confident. But as he walked next door his shoulders sagged dejectedly and he kept his head right down, not looking at anyone.

I glared at the crowd. There were now about forty people thronging around. Sarah's dad was ranting on to anyone who would listen about 'our public duty', while a grim-faced Sarah stood beside him. I could even feel a tiny bit sorry for her.

Then I saw the other man from the local authority – the one who'd done most of the talking – dart into the van. I went over. Inside the van I saw a large cage. Was that cage meant for Simon? I looked at the man in alarm. As if reading my thoughts he jumped down and closed the van door. I think that was his little gesture to show he knew Simon wasn't dangerous.

I asked him, 'Have you still got the photograph?'

'Yes.'

'Could I have it, please . . . it is mine, you know.'

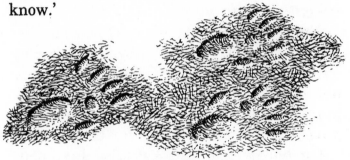

He hesitated, then handed it to me. 'Be very careful what you do with it, won't you?' he said.

'Oh I will,' I replied.

I was running into my drive when a bald-headed man from the crowd called out, 'Let's have a look at your picture, girlie.'

I shook my head and thrust the photograph down my pocket.

'You can make some money with that picture,' he went on.

'Leave her alone,' demanded an oddly commanding voice from the doorway. It was Nan.

I sped over to her. 'Did you see what happened, Nan?'

'I saw,' she replied bitterly, then she said, 'Let's go inside, shall we, love.' She said this so gently I was quite shocked. For she wasn't usually a very cosy Nan, to be honest.

I made Nan a pot of tea. My parents came back. 'There's someone from the zoo there now,' said Dad, 'and the police . . . I think they're going to be a while sorting all this out . . .' Then Jeff and his mum called in.

'I acted for the best,' said Jeff's mum. 'I really did.' She talked on and on again until finally Jeff stood up and announced, 'I want to apologize to Simon properly. Will you come with me, Kelly? We can tell him we've got the picture.'

'Sure, of course.'

But my dad said grimly, 'I don't think you'll get through. It's pandemonium out there.'

Dad was right. Now there were hordes of people jostling outside Simon's house. Where had they all come from? It was just like when there's a fight at school and hundreds of people suddenly appear out of nowhere. Only this crowd weren't yelling 'fight, fight, fight'; they were getting worked up about 'the unspeakable monster inside'. Several were waving cameras, while another was peering at the house through binoculars. How disgusting, I thought, until I remembered two nights ago I'd done exactly the same.

There was also a woman interviewing people in the crowd. I heard her call

out, 'Now, did anyone actually see this werewolf?'

Jeff and I pushed our way through. A policeman was now standing outside the door.

'Please let us in,' I said. 'We've got to see Simon.'

'Ah, everyone wants to see him.'

'But we're friends of his,' I cried.

'We need to tell him something important,' added Jeff.

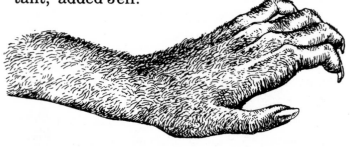

'I'm sorry,' said the policeman. 'But I've had strict instructions not to let anyone through at the moment.' Then he added, confidingly: 'There's a doctor in there; someone from the RSPCA; the local MP; while the boy's dad has just arrived . . . It's a real circus. Best talk to your friend tomorrow morning.'

We slowly walked back to my house. 'That's her,' cried a voice. 'She's the girl with a picture of the werewolf.'

The woman who'd been interviewing people sprang forward. She had a small, twitchy face and looked just like a hamster. 'Are you the girl who took the photo?'

'I might be.'

'Well, you've got a very valuable picture there. How about if I talk to you and your parents about it?'

'It's not for sale, is it?' said Jeff.

'That's right,' I replied.

We started to walk away.

'You're making a big mistake,' called the woman after us.

Seconds later she was ringing on the door-bell, demanding to talk to my parents and saying how I could name my own price. Mum soon got rid of her.

But Jeff said to me, 'I'm worried about that photograph . . . what if someone tries to steal it in the night? Who knows what people could do with it . . .? Then there would be pictures all over the place and you might have people turning up here wanting to do experiments on Simon.'

The photograph proved surprisingly difficult to tear up. In the end Jeff and I took it in turns to cut the photo up into the tiniest of pieces. At last I felt we were doing something to help Simon – and put things right.

'Tomorrow, most of the hair from Simon's face will have gone,' I said. 'In fact, it's probably disappearing now.'

'So Simon can go back to school just as before, can't he?' said Jeff eagerly.

'There'll be some fuss at first,' I replied. 'And some people might act a bit funny and treat Simon as some kind of outcast.'

'Well, I know what that's like,' said Jeff, 'so I can give him a few tips. I tell you what, I'll come round early tomorrow and we can make plans: the three of us.'

We shook hands and made a pact, that we would never let Simon down again.

CHAPTER ELEVEN

Next morning I was woken up by someone tapping on my bedroom door. Before I could reply the door opened.

'Are you awake, Kelly?' called a voice I recognized instantly.

'Yes, Nan . . . what time is it?'

'It's quite late,' snapped Nan. But my nan's 'quite late' equals 'very early' for most people. Nan always says if she stays in bed past six o'clock it gives her a headache. I was still feeling drowsy when Nan said, 'I've heard them next door. They're up and about and I think they'd appreciate a visit.'

I was out of bed at once then. For I was desperate to talk to Simon. Jeff and I had tried ringing him several times last night but the phone had been continually engaged.

I hurriedly had a shower and got dressed.

Then I helped Nan down the stairs. 'How's your ankle this morning, Nan?' I asked, politely.

'More important things to think about than that,' said Nan. She hated it if you asked her questions about her health. 'Do you want anything to eat?' she asked.

'No thanks, I'm not hungry . . . I just want to see Simon.'

Nan nodded in approval. 'I expect we'll be

offered a cup of tea next door anyway.'

Just as Nan was putting her hat on, Dad's sleepy voice called downstairs, 'Is everything all right?'

'What do you think?' snapped my nan, and closed the door before Dad could ask any more questions.

Outside there was a smaller crowd than last night. But there were still about fifteen people hanging about. A couple were passing flasks around. Another was setting up a video camera.

When they saw Nan and me come out of our house there was a buzz of interest. People looked at us expectantly as if we were actors on a stage. Then Nan raised her hand and cried, 'Out of my way, shoo, shoo,' as if they were chickens. I nearly burst out laughing.

The policeman had gone now. So Nan rang on the doorbell. Immediately all the dogs started barking. They sounded particularly angry and upset today. Then the door opened a crack. Mrs Doyle saw who it was and opened the door a little wider.

'Come in, come in,' she said, and as quickly

as Nan could manage we squeezed inside. Then the door was firmly closed again. The four dogs wagged their tails cautiously.

'We just came round to see how you are,' said Nan.

'How are we . . . yes, how are we?' Mrs Doyle appeared on the verge of tears. But then she recovered herself. 'We're all right, really . . . come and have a cup of tea in the kitchen.'

'That would be very nice,' said Nan.

There was no sign of Simon, but Mr Doyle was sitting on the stairs talking into his mobile phone. He nodded at us as we went past. He was talking very quickly so I couldn't catch what he was saying.

But then in the kitchen I saw two cases. I let out a cry, then looked up at Mrs Doyle.

'Yes,' she said, gently. 'We're leaving.'

'But why?' I began, then realizing that was a silly question, I went on, 'I mean, I know why, but we can fight this. Jeff and I will go to school with Simon today . . . and we'll talk them round. You'll see.'

'I'm not sure how many other pupils will be there,' said Mrs Doyle dryly. 'The headmaster rang me last night; he was very nice about it, but he's had calls all evening from parents saying they will remove their children from school while someone who is a dangerous werewolf – as they persist in calling Simon – is attending.'

'But once they know the truth . . .' I exclaimed.

'At the moment they're just not listening,' said Nan, settling herself at the kitchen table.

'But they've got to listen,' I cried.

'And they will. In time,' said Mrs Doyle. 'We had someone from the government round here last night. They've known about wolf-men and all the wonderful things they've done for years. I told them it's time everyone knew the truth. He said he agreed with me, so some good might come out of this.'

'Where's Simon?' I asked suddenly.

'He's upstairs, packing,' replied Mrs Doyle. 'He's quite upset about all this,' she added quietly.

'Could I see him?' I asked.

'Best to leave him now,' replied his mum, gently. 'But I know he'll be coming round to see you to say goodbye.'

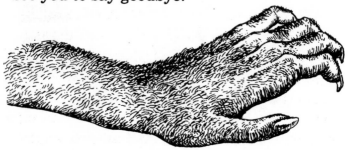

Goodbye. The word hammered away in my head blocking out everything else.

Later Nan and I walked back to my house. Nan seemed to be walking much more slowly now, her face almost touching mine. Tears started escaping down my face. 'Now what are you crying for?' said Nan indignantly. 'You've known a wolf-boy. There are very few human beings who can say that. You've been very lucky.'

'But Nan, he's leaving.'

'I know. But he has to go,' said Nan. 'For he wouldn't have much of a life here at the moment, would he? But he'll find you again. I am absolutely certain of that.'

Waiting in the doorway was Jeff. 'I couldn't sleep. How's Simon?' I didn't need to reply.

Jeff and I sat round the table pretending to eat breakfast. Neither of us could eat a thing. But we talked and talked . . . about Simon.

And then I had a terrible thought: what if Simon wanted to leave without saying goodbye to me? What if he was still angry with me? Was that why he hadn't come downstairs when I called?

I rushed to the front door. No; their car was still there. I watched Mr Doyle put some cases in the boot.

Then Mrs Doyle appeared with a bag. And finally, to my great relief, I spotted Simon.

There was a puzzled murmur of interest from the crowd as Simon jauntily strolled

171

through them in his T-shirt and jeans. 'That can't be him,' called a voice. For practically all the hair had disappeared from his face. Now he just had a few bits of stubble on his chin, while his hands were hidden again in black gloves.

'Are you the werewolf?' shouted someone after him. Simon didn't appear to hear. And then I saw why; he had his headphones on. With something of a flourish he took the headphones off. 'Just came round to say cheerio for now,' he announced to Jeff and me.

'Are you the werewolf?' shouted someone again. This time Simon heard him. There was an awkward silence for a moment. Then

Simon grinned. 'Got them really confused, haven't I?'

Inside I said, 'I quite miss all your hair now.'

'Did it all just go at once?' asked Jeff.

Simon didn't seem at all embarrassed by the question. 'Pretty much . . . you get this tickling sensation on your face and down your back . . . goes on for about an hour. But it's a laugh too. Like shaving without having to switch on the razor.' He grinned at us again. 'Anyway, I'm afraid I've got to go in a minute.'

Jeff went over to Simon. 'I'd like to shake you by the hand,' he said.

Simon immediately extended a gloved hand. Jeff shook his head. Understanding, Simon took off one of his gloves. The thick, black hair and pointed fingernails were still there. And seeing them so suddenly again made me catch my breath. Just for second. But Jeff didn't show any hesitation at all. He clasped Simon's hand firmly. 'Look after yourself then,' he said.

'And you,' replied Simon.

Then Simon said goodbye to my mum and

dad and Nan – who gave him her address if he should ever be passing – after which they all left to see off Simon's parents.

Now Simon and I were on our own.

'I wish you weren't going,' I cried.

'I'll be back before you know it,' said Simon lightly. 'Soon people will know the truth about wolf-boys and how incredibly cute and lovable we are.'

'Modest too.'

He laughed, then dug into his pocket and produced a little box. 'And this is for you.'

I stared at the box for a moment.

'Open it then,' said Simon.

Inside was the medal belonging to Simon's great-grandad. I read again the words: AWARDED TO SIMON GARSON FOR BRAVERY OCTOBER 1919.

'But I can't take this,' I gasped.

'I reckon if my great-grandad had heard what you said to that crowd last night, the way you . . . well I know he'd want you to have it. And so do I.'

'Oh, Simon, it's the most wonderful present I've ever had.'

'Is it really?' He looked pleased. 'Anyway

I'd better go. Don't forget me, will you?'

Outside a man in a yellow anorak stopped Simon. 'You live next door to it?' said the man. 'So you must know what animal is in there.' He nodded at Simon's house.

'All right, I'll tell you,' said Simon. 'It's a giraffe.'

'Not really,' exclaimed the man, excitedly.

Simon turned round and winked at me.

Five minutes later Simon was sitting in the back of his car with the four dogs scrambling over him.

The car drove quickly away.

I ran after it, waving frantically. Simon opened the window. 'Look out for giraffes – and a wolf-boy,' he called.

And then the car vanished around a corner.

He was gone.

I could feel tears pricking at the back of my eyes. I felt so sad and alone until I remembered . . . *Look out for a wolf-boy.* That's what Simon had called out to me. He would find me again, wouldn't he, just like Nan said.

'Hurry back, Simon,' I whispered. And then I let out this great long howl. Simon was far, far away by now. But somehow I knew he'd heard me.

THE END

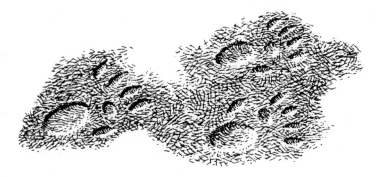

THE PHANTOM THIEF

Illustrated by Peter Dennis

This book is dedicated to:
Jan, Linda, Robin, Harry and Adam;
and Anne Everall.

CHAPTER ONE

I don't scare easily.

I wanted to tell you that first because, well, lately, something very strange has been happening to me.

And I've been scared out of my wits.

It started just the other day when I was sent to the padded cell.

Mr Crumble (we call him Crumbly) made me walk in front of him. He kept one hand on my shoulder all the way, as if he was afraid I'd try and escape. The padded cell was right at the end of the corridor.

I'd never been in there before. No-one from my class had. I was the first. It was a weeny little room: dark and cold. There were broken chairs stacked up at the back, an ancient blackboard, a window about the size of my thumbnail and a wooden desk and chair for the prisoner.

'You can sit down.' Crumbly spoke very quietly. And his lips never moved.

'Now you are here for some training in your own time.' That's what he calls detentions: training. He told us that anyone whose name appears in his black book – 'the naughty book' – three times will have extra training. Since September, five people from my class have got their names in the naughty book once. No-one has been in there twice. And only one name appears three times. Mine.

But he's always watching me: just waiting to pounce. You ask anyone.

Crumble handed me a piece of paper. I had to write I MUST BEHAVE PROPERLY IN CLASS on both sides. That didn't seem too bad until I saw it was graph paper with hundreds of micro lines. If I missed even one line out I would be back here for more training tomorrow.

Crumbly paced around the room while I

wrote. Every so often he would lean over my shoulder. I could hear him frowning. He's got a grey moustache which exactly matches his grey suit. And none of his suits fit him properly. They are far too baggy. I'm sure he buys them at jumble sales.

He said: 'I have to go but I shall return very shortly. On no account are you to leave this detention room. Do you understand, Alfred?' (Everyone else in the whole universe calls me Alfie).

When he says my name he pronounces every syllable. 'Al – f – red.' I can mimic his voice. Once I did an impression in the classroom. It sounded exactly like him. Everyone was in stitches until they spotted him in the doorway. He didn't say anything. But he knew I was taking him off.

The next day I told a joke in his lesson. Mrs

Macey, my teacher last year, always used to laugh at my jokes, but he made me stand on my chair and told the class to laugh at me. He was trying to make a show of me. Then he said he was tired of the way I kept turning round to see if I'd got a reaction. So now my place is right at the back. None of my mates sit anywhere near me now.

I should have been writing my lines. Instead I sat staring up at all the cobwebs. There was a little forest of them around the light. And it had turned very quiet. It was as if someone had turned the volume right down. Not a sound. I didn't like it. It was kind of eerie.

It seemed as if everyone else had gone. That I was the only person left in the school. I picked up my pen and started to write. I love making up stuff. I can write stories for hours. I had this idea. I started writing.

A spaceship has landed. And the aliens have

sent everyone to sleep, except me. The aliens had forgotten about me in here. But not for long, as they've got supersonic hearing. They can hear a crisp packet being opened from a hundred miles away.

And moments later they burst into the padded cell. Soon it's full of aliens. They all have short spikey haircuts (hedgehog haircuts we call them), goofy-looking noses, jug ears and cheeky grins. In other words, they look exactly like me.

'We've come to take you back,' they said. 'Your real home is actually in another dimension on another planet. You've been trapped down on Earth long enough. Come and join us and be happy for the rest of your life.' I didn't argue. But I decided I'd better leave Crumbly a note.

'Dear Mr Crumble, I am off to my real home up there in the sky, far away from you. If I don't see you again I'll remember the good times.

This will take me no time at all, as there weren't any.'

I stopped writing. I gazed down in horror at what I'd done. I'd filled up both sides of Crumbly's graph paper with my story. He'd go mad when he read it. What could I say? My pen took my hand hostage. I could never let him see it. I shivered. It was getting cold in here.

I'd have been freezing if I hadn't been wearing my new jacket. A black bomber jacket.

I chose it. It has orange lining which is the best lining you can get. Mum wanted to put my name in it. She had this horrible cotton label all ready. But that would have made me look a right mummy's boy. In the end I let her sew the label inside one of my pockets. No-one would ever see it there, but it kept her happy.

I drew my jacket around me. It was too cold to write. Perhaps that could be my excuse. My fingers had gone numb.

I practised making my fingers look stiff. Then I looked up and nearly jumped out of my skin.

There was someone else in the room

A boy who looked exactly like me.

CHAPTER TWO

I gaped at him in amazement. Had I conjured
him up? Had he wandered out of my story?

Now I was being daft. But I hadn't heard the
door open. I just looked up, and there he was.
Still, sometimes when I'm thinking hard I
don't hear things.

The boy didn't move any nearer to me. He
just stood by the door looking bewildered, as if
he couldn't quite believe he was there. He was
wearing our hideous, green uniform. Strange
I'd never seen him before.

15

'Hello,' I said at last. 'What do you want?'

He didn't answer. He just looked very puzzled. Finally I walked over to him. Up close he didn't look so much like me. He was quite a bit smaller. And his hair was much longer. It looked like a bush. And he didn't smile at all. He was very serious.

He must be new. He'd been sent here as a joke.

'Are you new?' I asked.

He opened his eyes wide. But he didn't answer. I wondered suddenly if he was an exchange student from France or Germany. A group came over in the summer. Maybe he was from another one? If so, it was a bit mean directing him in here. Were some boys sniggering outside? I couldn't hear anyone.

'Do you speak English?' I asked.

'Yes,' he said, slowly. 'And I am in Mrs Porter's class.'

'Mrs Porter,' I repeated. 'There's no teacher here called that, I'm afraid. Still, I'm always getting people's names wrong. Perhaps you mean Mrs Macey. She was my teacher last year.'

He shrugged helplessly.

'Don't worry about it,' I said. 'Actually, you're not supposed to be here at all. This is the detention room, the padded cell we call it. I was sent here by this really mean teacher . . .'

Suddenly he swayed forward as if he was going to faint. I darted towards him and pushed him on to my chair. For a moment he sat there with his head in his hands. I didn't know what to do. Should I get help?

Then he started muttering something. I couldn't make out what he was saying. I crouched down. He was shivering. His face was deathly pale.

I heard him say: 'Need help.'

'You need help?' I prompted.

He looked up. He had the same large blue eyes as me. He looked so unhappy I felt sorry for him. I wanted to help. He seized hold of my sleeve.

'In danger.' I made out those two words. But I couldn't hear any more. His teeth were chattering too much. I felt uneasy. There was something wrong here. Something bad.

A shudder ran through me.

I got up. 'I'm going to get someone.'

He struggled to speak.

'It's all right. I'll get Mrs Macey. She's good at first aid and things. I won't be long. OK?

He didn't answer, just sat there shivering.

'It's freezing in here, isn't it?' I said. Suddenly, impulsively, I handed him my jacket. 'Borrow this for a sec.'

He stared at me uncertainly. 'It's all right. It won't bite you. Bung it on . . . it's a good jacket, isn't it? There, that should stop you freezing to death . . . Oh yeah, what's your name?'

This time he answered at once: 'Alfred.'

That gave me a real start. 'But that's incredible. You've even got the same name as me. Only everyone calls me Alfie – perhaps they call you Alfie too?'

But somehow he looked more like an 'Alfred'.

Suddenly he sat bolt upright. 'Alfie,' he cried really urgently. I think he wanted me to stay. I hesitated. But then another shudder ran through me. I wanted someone else in on this.

'Don't worry, I'll be back before you know it. Take it easy.'

I opened the door carefully. If they gave trophies for lurking, Crumble would have a shelf full of them. He was always lying in wait in the darkest part of the corridor: ready to jump out at you. I looked both ways as if I was about to cross the road. All clear. I thought some boys might be hovering: the ones who'd lured Alfred into the padded cell. Surely he wouldn't have wandered in there on his own.

And who was he? Still, the main thing for me was to get him help.

I scuttled along the corridor. Crumble could pop up at any moment. I hovered outside the staffroom. Mrs Macey was usually in the staffroom at lunchtime as she was quite old, and walked with a limp. Sometimes she'd sit with her feet on another chair. Please let her be in there today.

I decided not to knock on the door just in case Crumble was in there. I'd just take a quick peek. The staffroom door creaked open. Now I could see. The staffroom was empty except for one person. He had his back to me. He was taking some books out of a cupboard. I recognized the ill-fitting suit instantly.

Then I did something stupid: I panicked and let go of the door. It slammed shut with a bang that made me jump a foot into the air.

I fled back down the corridor.

I ran fast – I came seventh in cross-country out of the whole school – but not fast enough.

'Alfred Drayton.'

The words hissed down the corridor after me.

CHAPTER THREE

Mr Crumble was pointing his finger at me. It was only a few centimetres away from my nose. There were yellow stains on the tips of his fingers. That's because he smokes so much.

'Who gave you permission to leave the detention room?'

He never raised his voice, even when he was really angry – like now.

Instead his voice was even softer, so it was hard to make out what he was saying.

'There's a boy in the padd . . . the detention room,' I began.

'What boy?'

'He's a new boy, and he's called . . .'

'There's no new boy here today.'

'Oh, OK then,' I stuttered. 'Well, I've never seen him before but he looks really ill. I came to get him some help.'

Mr Crumble screwed his eyes up and peered down at me beneath his bushy eyebrows. He often does that when I'm talking to him. Then he said something I couldn't catch – maybe I wasn't meant to? – and started marching down the corridor.

Crumble thought I was messing about. He thought there wouldn't be anyone in there. I was about to prove him wrong. Then he'd have to say I'd done a good deed. It might even turn out I'd saved Alfred's life. That would be great.

Crumble opened the door. At first all I could see was Crumble's back. Then I heard him give this loud sniff of annoyance. I peeped over his shoulder.

I couldn't believe what I saw – or rather didn't see.

For Alfred had vanished.

I was so shocked I forgot to breathe.

How could Alfred have left without me seeing – or hearing anything? I'd only been a few

metres away up the corridor. Besides, I
doubted if Alfred could have tottered to the
door on his own never mind wander off somewhere.

So where was he? People don't just melt
through walls. I stared hopelessly around me.
Crumble was prowling about too. He snatched
up my story about aliens: 'Are these your
lines?'

'Yes. No. Well, in a way.' Then I remembered
that rude letter I'd written at the end of the
story: 'Actually, it's private. Very private.'

Crumble didn't answer. He just went on
reading. His greasy skin shone under the light.
I stood stock still. I didn't know what to do.

At last Crumble stopped reading: 'Well,
what's happened to your sick boy?'

My face burned. 'I don't know.'

'It's a real mystery.'

'Yes.'

'Maybe this boy was an alien?'

I looked at him in amazement.

'And maybe this alien could change shape so he turned into a beetle and escaped under the door?'

Crumble does that sometimes: makes these really dry, sarcastic kind of jokes. So if you get an answer wrong in class he'll mutter, 'It'd be easier teaching fish to read.' He thinks he's funny. He's about as funny as a cup of cold sick.

'You have wasted my time and your time,' said Crumble.

'There really was someone here,' I said.

Crumble ignored this. 'So you will undertake extra training at home tonight. This time you have four sides of lines to complete.'

'But that's not fair,' I began.

'It's your own fault – you've brought it on yourself,' murmured Crumble. 'It seems to me you've been watching too much television,

24

with all this silliness about aliens and phantom boys.'

A phantom. Was that what Alfred had been? Yet, he hadn't been at all shadowy or misty. And my hand didn't go through him when I helped him on to a chair.

He'd looked as real and as solid as me.

Only a lot less healthy. Then I remembered something else: something terrible.

That ghost or whatever he was had stolen my jacket.

CHAPTER FOUR

It takes me exactly nineteen minutes to walk home from school. I've timed it.

Of course if I run I can do it in half that time. But I don't often run home these days.

Today it took me fifty-six minutes to get home. That was because I went for a walk. I needed to think about what had happened at lunchtime. But it didn't help. Afterwards I was as confused as ever.

People can't just disappear.

It didn't make any sense.

I threw my bag across the floor. I was fed up.

My mum appeared. 'At last. Where have you been?'

Centuries ago I used to tell my mum everything about my day. But not now.

'Just here and there,' I said.

'And Alfie, look at your shoes,' exclaimed Mum. 'Did you spend the whole day wading in the mud? Take them off at once, then come into the kitchen.'

I flung my shoes into the shoe-box, then went into the kitchen. Mum was sitting at the table. Her glasses were perched on top of a pile of papers. She teaches at the college in the town.

'Sit down, Alfie.' Something was wrong, I could tell. 'I've just had your teacher on the phone.' I swallowed hard. Crumble strikes again. 'He tells me you ran out of his detention.'

'I didn't run out.'

'You said you'd seen an alien.'

I shook my head, 'That man is such a liar.'

'He said that instead of writing your lines you wrote a story about an alien who looked like you. Then you pretended the alien had turned up and needed help.'

'No, no.'

'All right,' said Mum. 'Tell me your side of it.'

I hesitated. 'It's hard to explain.'

'Did you write a story instead of doing the lines, as you were told?'

'Well, yes.'

'And did you leave the detention room?'

'Yes . . . but . . . I had no choice.' Mum looked at me expectantly. 'This boy turned up.'

'In the detention room?'

I nodded. 'And he was pretty ill, so I went to get help. But when I came back with Crumble the boy had gone.'

'Who was he?'

'I don't know. I've never seen him before.'

Mum sighed.

'It's all right you sighing,' I said, 'it was a very eerie experience.'

'What was?' asked Rachel from the doorway.

'Nothing to do with you,' I muttered. Rachel's my sister and she used to be all right. She had an earring in her nose, stayed out late every night and was always rowing with Mum. Sometimes I'd wake up at night and hear them screaming at each other. It was excellent. But lately Rachel's changed. She goes on and on about her exams and what grades she's hoping to get. She works for hours in her room every night.

Worse still, she and Mum have become all pally, going off shopping, then sitting together on the couch giggling over what they've bought. It's disgusting to watch.

And while Rachel just used to ignore me, now she's always nagging me about something. It's like I've suddenly gained another parent. (Just to let you know, my dad left home shortly after I was born. He's now got another family in Dublin. I haven't seen him for years. He sends me good presents on my birthday, though.)

'You're not in trouble again, are you?' demanded Rachel.

'Alfie's school rang up,' explained Mum. 'He didn't do his detention.'

'Don't tell her,' I said. 'It's none of her business.'

But Rachel had already pulled up a chair. 'That's all you need, isn't it, Mum?' She turned to me. 'Mum's been on her feet all day and she's back in the college this evening. Surely you can at least try and behave at school?'

'Like you did, you mean? Mum was always having to go up to the school about you.'

'That's enough,' said Mum.

'You're just so ungrateful,' said Rachel. 'Mum went out specially last week with you to get you a new jacket and this is how you repay her.'

Mum was looking curiously at me now. 'Where is your jacket, Alfie? You weren't wearing it when you came in.'

I stared miserably back at her. 'I loaned it to someone.'

'Who?' demanded Mum.

'That boy in the detention room, actually.'

'No, Alfie,' cried Mum. 'This really won't do. When you were younger it might have been funny to make up all these stories – but not now.'

31

'You've lost it, haven't you?' taunted Rachel.

'No, I'll get it back.'

'You'd better,' said Mum. 'I'm not buying you another one; that's got to last you the entire year.'

'We're not made of money, you know,' hissed Rachel.

'Just shut your mouth,' I hissed back. I didn't want to stay in this house another second. I'd go round to Grandad's. I could tell him what had happened. And perhaps he could even explain it. I got up.

'Where are you going?'

'I'm going to Grandad's,' I said. 'I'll have my tea round there.'

'Sit down,' said Mum. 'Before you do anything else, you'll finish those lines for Mr Crumble.'

When I showed Mum the graph paper he'd given me she did say, 'Oh, they're such small lines,' and a look of sympathy crossed her face. But then she said, briskly, 'Still, the sooner you start the sooner you finish.' After which, another bombshell: 'Oh yes, Mr Crumble said they are still looking for pupils to help at the Open Evening tomorrow, so I volunteered you.'

'You did what?'

Mum started to laugh. 'Now don't look so horror-struck, it won't do you any harm . . . and besides, you were at the last Open Day.'

'Yes, but then I was playing in the football demonstration. This time I'll be showing parents round. Only gimps do that.'

'Honestly,' said Rachel, 'why do you have to make such a fuss about everything? And I don't suppose Alfie's brought the logs in for the fire like he's supposed to.'

'I haven't had a chance,' I snapped.

'It's all right, I'll do it,' she said.

'Oh, are you sure, dear?' asked Mum.

Rachel gave her martyr's smile. 'No problem at all, Mum.'

'Creep,' I muttered at her. 'And I'm not going to that poxy Open Evening tomorrow,' I muttered under my breath.

'Oh yes you are,' replied Mum. 'I know you won't let me down.'

It was after seven when I finally escaped to Grandad's. It was a windy, drizzly October evening. Mum made me wear my old grey coat. She had chosen it for me and she's got terrible taste. It's even got a hood. I can't stand hoods, they're so babyish. I'd rather take a hat with me.

I took a short-cut to Grandad's down the alleyway. Mum doesn't like me going this way as there are no street lights. But tonight I was in a hurry.

Thick bushes crouched on either side of the pavement. Their leaves rustled in the wind. Suddenly I stopped. I had the strangest feeling someone was following me. It wasn't anything I'd heard. I just sensed it. I turned round. The darkness was full of shadows. Did one of those shadows move?

I began to walk faster. Was the person behind me walking faster too? A pile of dead

leaves flew up into the air. They made a strange, whooshing noise. It sounded eerie. I should have looked round again. But I was too scared at what I might see.

Instead, I shouted down the alley, 'Oh, there you are, at last.'

And I ran all the way to Grandad's, my breathing hissing in my ears. Then I tried to laugh at myself. But to be honest, I still felt shaken up.

Grandad's house stands back from the road behind a large hedge. He lives there with Molly, his dog. I rang on the doorbell. Usually Molly would be barking and sniffing at the door and I'd be telling her not to worry, it was only me.

But today, the house was horribly silent. And the only sound was Grandad undoing the chain and opening the door.

'Well, if it isn't young Alfie,' he said. My grandad is both young and ancient. He's got a bald, shiny head ('My hair is very seldom,' he says: that's one of his little mildewed jokes) and wears glasses with ugly, black frames. He dresses old, too: grey v-necked pullovers, brown trousers, sports jacket, and when he goes out a flat cap. (I really like his cloth cap though. He lets me borrow it sometimes.)

But my grandad also wears trainers – he says normal shoes can't support his feet. And he can move really fast in his trainers. In fact, from a distance you wouldn't think he was old at all.

'How are you, Alfie?' he asked.

'Terrible – I'm in trouble with Mr Crumble about . . .'

'If I had a pound for every time you've said that I'd be sunning myself in the Bahamas,' interrupted Grandad. 'I suppose you're going to tell me about it.'

I grinned at him. 'That's right, and I want to ask your opinion about something important.'

'Come in. We're in the study.'

'How's Molly?'

'Ah, she doesn't know she's born, sitting around all day, being carried everywhere. I told her not to get used to this.'

Grandad gave a kind of chuckle. But I wasn't fooled.

Molly's been Grandad's dog for nearly six years. After Nan died Grandad hardly went out. Mum thought a dog would help him get out again. I went with Grandad to the kennels where he first saw Molly. A black labrador.

She came right up to the edge of the dog cage.
I knew she wanted us to take her: 'Now, that's
a dangerous dog,' said Grandad, 'because if you
let her, she'll break your heart.'

She settled in at Grandad's right away. And
both Grandad and I would take her for long
walks. It was just perfect until recently a bone
in Molly's back became loose. The vet said it
was too dangerous to remove it. And poor old
Molly's back legs became paralysed.

The vet said it might be easier for Grandad
if Molly was put down. And even my mum
thought it would be too much for Grandad
lifting Molly about everywhere.

But Grandad just said, 'She can use two legs,
can't she – and that's as many as me.' Then
this girl, Sarah, who lives next door to
Grandad saw a photograph of a dog in a special
dog trolley. It was in an American magazine.
And Grandad sent away for one for Molly. He
filled in this great long form giving all of

Molly's measurements. Now he was waiting for the trolley to arrive.

Molly was lying in her basket. Grandad had put it by the fire as that was her favourite spot. When she saw me she barked and thumped her tail. Usually I crouch beside Molly and sit stroking her for hours. I can hear her whimpering under her breath and I tell her not to worry; she'll be back on her feet again soon. But Molly just gives me this look, as if to say I've heard that before.

But today there was someone else stroking her: Sarah. She goes to my school. She's in my class, in fact. But I never speak to her. No-one does. Because she's dead weird. She hasn't got any friends – except for Grandad. She only moved next door to Grandad a few months ago. But she's got well-in with him and Molly already. She's always round their house now. It really annoys me.

Grandad brought in a jug of orange juice and a large plateful of biscuits. He told us to tuck in. In the past Molly would get up on her hind legs to beg for food. Today she just stared mournfully at us. I ended up giving her practically all of my biscuits.

'Look at that dog, she's getting thoroughly spoilt,' said Grandad. Then he asked me what I wanted to talk to him about. He didn't seem to realize that a stranger was there. I hesitated.

'Do you want me to go?' asked Sarah, staring at the carpet.

I did, very much. But I didn't think I could say that out loud. Then Grandad said, 'Well, young Alfie's in trouble again with Mr Crumble.'

'Oh, I know all about that,' she said, dismissively.

Stung by her tone I said, 'I don't think you do, actually.' But I wasn't going to say any more about what had happened with Crumble. That was personal. Instead, I said, 'Anyway, it's not exactly about that: Grandad, do you believe in things like ghosts?'

'Not at all,' said Grandad, so confidently I was quite surprised.

'But lots of people see them,' I said.

'Ah, but then imagination is a mighty powerful thing,' said Grandad. 'But that's all they are: a trick of the mind.'

I looked at him doubtfully.

'Listen, Alfie, if I said I saw little green ghosts outside the old church, within hours lots of other people would say they had seen them too. And they would think they had. But only in their minds.'

'So no ghost really exists?'

'Absolutely not,' said Grandad. 'There's a perfectly rational explanation for every ghost story.' Grandad was so firm about this I didn't know what to say next.

Then Molly started to bark and look at the door. 'Want to go out, do you girl?' asked Grandad. 'Off we go, then.' He put the special harness around Molly and picked her up. 'You two can finish off the biscuits while we're gone . . . but save one of the chocolate ones for me, or there'll be trouble.' Molly barked again. 'All right, girl, I'm going as fast as I can.'

After Grandad left the only sound was the fire crackling and hissing and Grandad's clock ticking away. I began to think about what Grandad had said.

When I thought I was being followed – well that could have been a trick of the mind, I suppose. But what about the boy in the padded cell? I couldn't just have imagined him. And what about my jacket. Where on earth had that gone?

'I believe in ghosts,' said Sarah, suddenly.

I looked up, shocked. I'd sat in this room with Sarah a number of times but we'd never said anything to each other, except a muttered 'hello'.

'Oh, do you?'

'And you've just seen a ghost, haven't you?'

I gazed at her, stunned. 'Why do you say that?'

She gave a strange kind of smile. 'But I'm right, aren't I?'

CHAPTER FIVE

'Yes, all right,' I said, 'I have seen a ghost. I saw it today, actually.'

There was definitely a flicker of envy in Sarah's eyes now. 'Where did you see it?' she demanded.

'In the padded cell.'

'The what?'

'The detention room.'

'Actually, padded cells don't have any furniture in them so you shouldn't really call it . . .'

'Do you want me to carry on with my story or not?'

Sarah looked huffy. 'Go on then.'

'This boy came in, about my age, looked a little bit like me. And he was pretty ill. Well if he was dead, I suppose he was very ill indeed.'

Not even the tiniest smile from Sarah.

'How do you know he was a ghost?' she asked.

'By the way he just disappeared. I went up the corridor to get help and when I got back he'd gone . . . vanished.'

'And he hadn't climbed out of the window?'

'An ant could just about climb out of that window. Nothing any bigger.'

'And there was no other way of escape?'

'No.'

'Not a trap door, or anything.'

'Oh yes, there was, actually. Dirty great thing. I popped down it myself.'

'There's no need to be sarky.'

'But what a stupid question.'

'I must explore every possibility,' she said.

'And you've got to remember that I know far more about ghosts than you. I've read more than fifty books about them.'

'But I've seen one.'

'You *think* you've seen one,' she corrected. 'Now tell me again what happened and don't miss out a single detail – then I'll let you know if you've seen a real ghost or not.'

At that point I nearly walked out. I nearly went out and joined Grandad and Molly in the garden. Talk about big-headed. No wonder no-one liked her.

But I didn't want to keep this story to myself any more. It was actually a relief to tell someone, even if it was the Smurf. That's what everyone in my class calls Sarah, because she's very small . . . and very annoying.

All the time I was talking, Sarah sat staring into the fire. She didn't look at me once until I'd finished.

'I've heard you make up stories,' she said.

'Have you?'

'Is this one of them?'

'You're the great ghost detective. You tell me.'

'Despite everything, I believe you,' she said, finally. 'I think you've seen a true ghost.'

A shiver ran through me.

'It's a well-known fact,' went on Sarah, 'that ghosts often haunt a place where something happened to them. Usually something bad.'

'Maybe Crumble murdered him in there?'

She sighed. 'Now you're just being silly again.'

'No more silly than you and your trap door.'

She ignored this. 'I expect the boy died in that room of some terrible disease. Now he keeps returning to the room. He can't help himself. I think we should go back there and wait for him.'

I looked up. 'We?'

'Yes, you'll need me as a witness. I can prove what you say – and show you're not going round the bend.'

'Well, thanks . . . but we can't just wander into the padded cell and say we're waiting for a ghost. Teachers would never allow it.'

She shook her head impatiently. 'Tomorrow night is the ideal time.'

'Tomorrow night?'

'Yes, during the parents' evening. When everyone is in the hall we can slip away to the detention room and watch for your ghost.'

That was such a good idea I was ashamed I hadn't thought of it.

'I've volunteered to help tomorrow,' she said, 'although I'm quite certain you haven't.'

'Well, that's where you're wrong,' I replied, enjoying the look of surprise on her face. 'Me, I never miss a good parents' evening.'

Before she could reply, Grandad and Molly had returned. I sat there, planning it all out. I certainly would ghost-watch in the padded cell tomorrow night. And I'd have someone with me as a witness, too.

Only it wouldn't be the Smurf.

CHAPTER SIX

It seemed strange walking back to school in the evening in my school uniform.

I arrived just as Mrs Macey was giving out our name tags. I was glad Mrs Macey was in charge tonight, not Mr Crumble. She was all right.

She was telling us what to do. But she kept fiddling with her buttons. Teachers always get nervous on parents' evenings.

She said we had to go up to each adult we saw and ask, very politely, if they would like to be escorted into the hall. Then we had to show them to a seat.

'Then can we put our hand out for a tip?' I asked.

'Just you dare,' said Mrs Macey. But she was laughing. You can have a joke with her. Practically everyone else smiled, except the Smurf, of course.

Sarah is skinny, and a bit spotty. She's got long, mousy hair, starey, green eyes, and she wears merit badges all down her blazer. You get merit badges for good work. I got some when I was in Mrs Macey's class. But I wear them on the inside of my blazer. You can wear them on the outside when you're about five. But not now. It just gives you a really bad image.

No wonder the other girls were giving Sarah dirty looks. I was glad I wasn't going to watch for the ghost with her. I looked around for

Michael. He was my best mate. Well, he still is. It's just I've hardly seen him since Crumble moved me to the back of the class.

He'll wait for that ghost with me all right. But there wasn't time to ask him as parents were already swarming about. This man with a face like a horse peered hopefully at me. 'Perhaps this young man can tell me where to go?' he said.

I didn't dare answer that one.

The next half hour was really busy. I amused myself by talking to the parents in different accents: Irish, Scottish, Brummy, and I even tried out an Italian one, although I don't think that was one of my biggest successes as the parents kept giving me odd looks. I have a feeling they won't be sending their children here.

Then I spotted Michael on his own. There was no time to mess about so I got straight into the subject.

'Hiya, Mike, do you believe in ghosts?'

'Not much. Why? Don't tell me, you've seen one.'

'As it happens, I have. And it's in this school, just upstairs in the padded cell.'

'In detention, is he?' said Michael grinning.

'No, he's . . . well, ghosts don't do a lot, do they? But he's up there, haunting away.'

'Oh, really,'

'No, listen, I've seen him . . .' I started to explain.

'Wind up, wind up,' interrupted Michael.

'No, it's not. I'm sure he's there and I just want a witness to come and see.'

He started backing away. 'No, sorry,' said Michael. 'I can't.'

'Why?'

'My mum and dad have promised me a new mountain bike for my birthday next week if I stay out of trouble.'

'Is that why you've hardly spoken to me lately?'

'No, of course not – it's just you're always in trouble with Crumble . . .'

'That's not my fault.'

'I know. But I've got other mates too.'

'And I hope you'll be very happy with them – and your new mountain bike.'

'Don't be like that,' said Michael. 'There isn't really a ghost upstairs, is there?'

'You'll never know now, will you?' I said and walked away.

I didn't care if I never spoke to him again.

Then I spotted Sarah. She was standing in the doorway with two other girls from my form. Most of the parents were in the hall now. They were waiting for any late-comers.

Mrs Macey rushed up. 'All right girls, and you, Alfie, . . . I think everyone's arrived, so you can come into the hall now. Sit quietly on the mats at the back.' She sped off again.

The two girls linked arms. They acted as if Sarah wasn't there, although I heard them mutter 'the Smurf' and then giggle. Sarah didn't react at all. Her face was a mask. Then she came over to me.

'I've just got to get something,' she said. 'Meet you at the top of the stairs . . .' she spoke out of the side of her mouth as if she was in a spy film.

'Yes, all right.' I supposed Sarah was better than no-one. Just.

And then she hissed after me: 'And don't let anyone see you.'

I just gritted my teeth in reply. Actually, the hall doors were closed so it was quite easy to sneak upstairs. I hovered around. All the classroom doors were open and inviting, while the walls were top-heavy with pictures. Only one door was firmly closed. No-one would be taken to the padded cell tonight. It was out of bounds for all visitors.

'Hello.'

I swung round. Sarah was beside me. She was carrying a large bag.

'Off on your holidays after this, are you?' I asked.

'I've brought our equipment,' she said.

'What equipment?'

'Oh, you'll see. Now hurry up, we haven't got a moment to lose.'

We half-ran down the corridor. The door to the padded cell loomed in front of us. I felt just a bit apprehensive.

'Do you think we should knock first in case the ghost's waiting for us?'

'Stop being silly and open the door,' said Sarah.

The door creaked open. Funny how I didn't remember it creaking in the day. I stared around me. I hate the way rooms grow in the dark. They stretch out for ever at night. Even midget rooms like this one.

I grabbed for the light switch. The room was lit up for one half second, then there was a pinging noise and thick darkness again.

'Bulb's gone,' said Sarah.

'Oh thanks for telling me. I'd never have guessed.'

Now, light bulbs explode all the time. The one on our landing went a couple of nights ago. That's the one my mum hates changing. So I did it for her.

Yet there seemed something ominous about it happening the moment we stepped in here. I started whistling under my breath. Soon my eyes would get used to the darkness. For now the room was full of dark shapes. Even Sarah was little more than a shadow.

I wished there was some kind of light in here. And then there was.

Sarah was waving a torch about. A pale, yellow light prowled restlessly around the room. It couldn't seem to settle. Little corners of the room were caught in its glare, just for a moment, before the light leapt on again. But there was nothing – or no-one here – I could see that. I should have begun to relax. But instead, my feeling of uneasiness grew.

Something wasn't right here. I knew it.

Finally I sat down at the prisoner's desk.

'Was that where you were sitting when you saw the ghost?'

Sarah's torch beamed in on me as I answered, 'That's right, this is the very spot.'

She sat down opposite me in the teacher's chair. Then out of her bag she produced a tape-recorder.

'What's that for? Going to interview the ghost, are you?'

'Maybe. Imagine if we got your ghost talking on tape.'

'He's not my ghost,' I muttered. 'I just happened to see him – and he's pinched my jacket. That's the first thing I'll ask him about.'

'I doubt he's actually stolen it,' said Sarah. 'Ghosts often move things about but they rarely keep them. Now, I've also brought some binoculars.'

'Sarah, we're in a weeny little room, not a field.'

'I know that,' said Sarah. 'But still, they could be useful if I want to get a closer look.'

'Don't tell me you've got a camera in there as well.'

'No point. Ghosts haven't got any reflection, have they?'

'How do you know that?'

'Oh it's a well-known fact. Ghosts can never be seen in mirrors so they can't be photographed either. I'll do my first report now.'

'But nothing's happened yet.'

'I know, but I just want to write up a few details.'

Then the only sound was her pen scratching over the page. She seemed to think this was some kind of adventure. I wished I felt the same way. But I didn't. I had the strangest feeling we shouldn't really be in here.

Sarah looked up. 'And you first saw the ghost

in the doorway, is that right?'

'Yes, I just looked up and there he was.'

In a moment would I look up and see him again? Would he come in here looking pale and ill, muttering about how he needed help again? I'd hate to be a ghost: just living the same piece of time over and over again. Could he never break free?

I sniffed. The room smelt old and musty. And then I heard something, a kind of rustling noise as if someone was folding up a newspaper. I looked up sharply. Sarah was still writing; one hand holding her torch. She obviously hadn't heard anything.

But then she called across to me. 'It's just the wind.'

'What is?'

'The noise that made you jump a moment ago; it's only the wind outside.'

'I know,' I said quickly.

'I think it's going to rain soon.'

'How fascinating.'

Sarah put her pen down, then I heard her whisper, 'Alfred.'

'My name's Alfie.'

'I'm not talking to you.'

'What?'

'I'm calling to Alfred. I can't wait any longer. I want to see him, Alfred . . . Alfred.'

A shudder ran through me. 'No, don't do that . . . don't call him up like that.'

'Why?'

'I don't know, exactly. I just don't think you should, because . . .' and then the breath caught in my throat. For I saw something move. Over in the corner of the room just by the blackboard there was a shape, a shadow. I wasn't exactly sure. But something was there. Was it him, Alfred, hiding in the shadows?

'What's wrong?' called Sarah. There was fear in her voice too.

'Over by the blackboard,' I cried. 'I saw something.'

'Is it Alfred?'

'I don't know.'

All at once Sarah was up and shining her torch about. I don't know why, but I felt she shouldn't.

'No, don't go over there . . . don't disturb it. I don't think it wants to be seen,' I whispered, frantically.

But Sarah was already over by the blackboard. 'There's nothing here,' she began. Then suddenly she let out this sharp cry and the torch just flew out of her hand. We were in darkness again.

'I hate you!' she yelled.

'Me, why?' I spluttered.

She didn't answer. Instead, she stumbled past and ran out of the door. I heard her feet padding furiously down the corridor. She sounded as if she was being chased by some great monster.

I started to breath in gulps. I didn't understand this. I staggered to my feet. I picked up her torch and waved it towards the blackboard.

And then I saw there was writing on the blackboard. Four words had been put down by some invisible hand. The words screamed out of the darkness at me.

YOU ARE IN DANGER.

CHAPTER SEVEN

YOU ARE IN DANGER. Where had those words come from? I didn't know. I just knew I had to get out of here. Somehow I managed to bundle up all Sarah's equipment first. I kept flicking the torch around me; its light seemed to keep whatever was in this room at bay.

Then I tore down the corridor. Where had Sarah gone? Had she run home? I had to talk to her. I wanted her to know that it wasn't me who had written that message. For that's what she'd assumed.

But also, I couldn't keep tonight locked away in my own head. I had to talk about this with someone – even if it was only the Smurf.

As I passed the hall I could hear clapping. But the parents' evening seemed far away from me. I had far more important things to think about now.

Outside, that musty smell from the padded cell still seemed to hang about me. I couldn't shake it off. I walked quickly, then froze. Sitting in the bus shelter across the road was Sarah. She had her head in her hands. She looked really miserable as if she'd just heard some terrible news. I crossed the road.

She never even noticed me. She didn't look up until I said her name.

'You forgot your bag,' I said.

She didn't answer, just glared fiercely at me.

I put the bag down beside her.

'Why did you run off like that?' I demanded.

She turned away. I thought she wasn't going to answer. I hate it when people sulk. My sister sulks. But then she hissed, 'You think you're so funny, don't you? Well, go on, tell all your friends you got me to believe your stupid story. You made a fool of the Smurf, all right.' She was breathing really fast when she spoke. She

made me feel guilty – even though I hadn't done anything.

'Sarah, I didn't write that message,' I said, in this very reasonable voice: the one I use when I think my mum's about to have a go at me. 'I promise you, I didn't do it. I mean, didn't you see how scared I was?' That made her look at me. She didn't say a word. But she moved up along the seat. I sat down beside her. 'Do you believe me?' I asked.

She considered. 'Maybe you wrote it subconsciously?'

'I hope not, because that would mean I was going a bit loony. And I don't think I am . . . Grandad says there's a rational explanation for everything. So in this case someone must have put that message up there as a joke.'

'Who?'

'I don't know. Someone with nothing better to do who wanted to scare the next person in the padded cell.'

'But no-one ever does lessons in there,' said Sarah. 'And I'm pretty certain the last person to have detention in there was you. It just doesn't make sense – unless . . .'

'Unless what?'

'Unless that ghost wrote it as a kind of warning to you, or me. Probably you.'

'Thanks.'

'Perhaps that ghost can see into the future?'

'If he can, I wish he'd tell me how Man United are going to do on Saturday.'

'Oh, be serious,' said Sarah.

'Yeah, but come on, it's not much of a message, is it? If he'd written "You will die if you eat school dinners tomorrow", then at least I'd know what to do. But his message is so vague, it's useless.'

'Maybe he writes that message every evening,' said Sarah.

'You mean each night this ghost wanders

into the padded cell, writes "You are in danger" on the blackboard, then spooks off until the next night, when he writes the same thing all over again.'

'It's the most likely explanation,' said Sarah.

'Well, all I can say is that ghost wants to get himself a life . . . that's a joke, by the way.'

'I know.'

'And would it have killed you to smile?'

'Oh, I hardly ever smile,' said Sarah. She got up. 'We haven't finished our investigation, have we? We should really go back and see if this ghost materializes – that's the proper word for ghostly appearances – and ask him about the message.'

'Yeah, all right.' But I didn't move. I really didn't want to go back to that room again. Not now. I studied my watch.

'The meeting will be over now, so parents will be all over the place – and teachers. It'll be hard to sneak into the padded cell now. There's bound to be someone who spots us.'

'That's true.' Was there a note of relief in Sarah's voice?

'To be honest,' – I gave this strange kind of laugh – 'I wonder if that ghost isn't best left alone . . .'

'What do you mean?'

I hesitated. 'Well, it's hard to explain, but every time I see him I get the feeling that, well, something's wrong – or about to go wrong.' I stopped. Sarah was staring intently at me. 'Stop looking at me in that tone of voice,' I said. 'And listen, if you do want to go back there, I will. After all, two's safer than one.'

'No, you're right,' began Sarah. 'It's too late to go back now.' She picked up her bag.

'Shame you never got to tape him, though.'

'Shame you never got your jacket back,' said Sarah. 'Still, I expect it will turn up. He'll have put it somewhere you haven't thought of yet.' Then she added in a low whisper, as if he might be listening, 'Some ghosts enjoy causing trouble and, yes, those ones are probably best left undisturbed.'

But next morning I returned to the padded cell. Daylight made me brave – and angry. How dare that ghost write such a pathetic message. I was going to march in there and rub out 'You are in danger'. That would show him.

My chance came just before school had properly started. I was helping Mrs Macey pack up after the Open Evening. She wanted to know where I'd disappeared to last night. I told her

Sarah hadn't been feeling very well and so I'd taken her home.

'That was very kind of you,' said Mrs Macey in a suspicious voice. But she didn't say anything else. She was too busy.

Then the phone rang in the staffroom. And she disappeared. While I shot down the corridor to the padded cell. I opened the door. The room had shrunk again to its normal, poky size. I went over to the blackboard. I had my hankie all ready. But there was no need.

The message had gone.

But who had rubbed it out?

No-one would have been in here yet. My heart started to thump.

There was something weird going on here. Even in the daytime.

I ran outside. I never wanted to go into that room again.

At breaktime I told Sarah what I'd done. Her

eyes opened wide when I told her the message had vanished.

'But that's good,' I said. 'It means I'm not in danger any more. It's all over.'

I kept telling myself that.

I certainly never expected to see that ghost again.

CHAPTER EIGHT

After school I took off on my bike. I like just cycling around. It's never boring. There's always something new to see. Besides, cycling helps me think. I thought about that ghost in the padded cell. Would it be writing 'You are in danger' on the blackboard again tonight? And would it rub the message off before daylight?

I'd never know because I wasn't going back to that room, ever.

When I returned Grandad's car was parked

in the drive. Grandad never called around at this time. Something must have happened.

Was Molly all right?

Grandad opened the door. He looked as if he'd been up all night. He looked terrible.

'Grandad . . . ?' But I didn't dare ask him about Molly. I was too scared of what he'd tell me.

'We've been waiting for you, young Alfie,' he said.

'Me, why?'

'We need your help,' replied Grandad, mysteriously.

I followed him into the kitchen. Mum was there. And Sarah. I started when I saw her. But my eyes were already searching for Molly. Grandad never went anywhere without her.

Then to my great relief I saw Molly. She was sitting in what looked like a small box on wheels. 'Is that the dog-cart?' I asked.

'That's right,' said Grandad. 'Arrived first

70

thing this morning.' He started explaining how it worked. The wheels took the place of her back legs. But her front legs were free to move around, although there was a little belt around her tummy so she couldn't fall out.

'But it's excellent,' I said. 'I bet Molly loves it, doesn't she?'

'I'm sure she will love it,' replied Grandad cautiously. 'But she's still getting used to it at the moment.'

'So how far has she gone in it?' I asked.

'Not very far,' admitted Grandad. 'In fact, she hasn't gone anywhere, yet. But it's not for want of trying.'

'Grandad's worn himself out,' began Mum. 'I thought that dog-cart was supposed to make life easier for you.'

Grandad brushed this comment away with a wave of his hand. 'This dog-cart takes a bit of understanding. I mean, we don't just sit on a bike and ride off, do we? Anyway we need all hands on deck for this one. I've had a go and so has Sarah here, but as you're the one who taught Molly all her tricks . . .'

'Yeah, I'll have a go. Of course I will,' I said. And it was true; I was the one who'd taught Molly to beg, jump for a tit-bit, get her lead, and to turn door handles. Molly could get into every room in Grandad's house before she became ill.

'Don't worry, leave it to me – the master dog-trainer,' I said.

I pushed Molly out into the back garden. Then I crouched down and started whispering to her. I always do that before I teach her a new trick. 'Molly, you've got wheels,' I said, 'and those wheels will take you where you want. You can go anywhere in the world again. Just trust me, all right?'

Molly sat there looking at me out of one eye. She does that when she doesn't want to do something. She thinks if she can't see you very clearly you can't see her either.

And she didn't move an inch. Grandad and Sarah crouched down beside me and started talking to her again. Then we'd take it in turns to tug at the dog-cart with the lead which was attached to it.

But still Molly wouldn't budge. Until finally she slumped forward and put her head in her paws. She couldn't see us at all now. And that was just how she wanted it.

'Ah well, she'll get it eventually. It's still early days,' said Grandad. But his face was lined with anxiety.

Mum came out. 'I've cooked you a meal, Dad,' she said.

'I couldn't eat a thing,' he replied.

'Now you won't be any use to Molly if you don't eat. So come inside and eat it up while it's still hot . . . the children will keep an eye on Molly.'

'I don't know,' grumbled Grandad. 'The day you retire everyone starts treating you just like a kid again.' But he followed Mum inside.

'Molly,' I whispered urgently.

Not even her ears twitched.

'It's no good,' I said.

And then Molly started to whimper to herself. She was upset and confused. Sarah immediately put her arm around Molly. 'Don't you worry. We won't make you do anything you don't want to do . . . She looks tired,' she continued. 'Maybe we should give her a break, let her go to sleep for a while?'

'No,' I replied firmly. Molly was sleeping more and more these days. She was acting as if she was a very old dog. That worried me. 'We'll push her around the garden.'

Molly didn't seem to mind this at all. We went right to the top of the garden. When we passed the old shed Molly got excited.

'She remembers,' I said. 'In the summer I'd be in this shed a lot. I took it over after Mum got a new one. And I kept dog-chocs in there, didn't I, Molly?'

Molly was staring intently at me now with her melting, brown eyes.

'Come on then, let's see if there are any chocs left for you.'

I helped Molly inside and discovered two dog biscuits which she immediately wolfed down. Sarah hovered outside.

'I'd better go,' she said.

'You don't have to. Come in.'

Sarah stepped inside, looking all around her as if she was stepping into a mysterious cave, not a tatty old shed.

'No-one, apart from Molly, has ever been inside here. This is my private place.'

'I like it,' said Sarah.

'Do you? Well I'll give you a quick tour. On the floor there,' I pointed, 'you will spy some very ancient comics and cycling magazines and a few games, while above you on the first shelf are some of my favourite books. The other shelf has only one thing on it: my cycling trophy. It's the only trophy I've ever won. I won it two years ago, so it's practically an antique now. But I'm hoping to have a twin for that trophy in a couple of weeks. I'm in this year's Junior Cycling Race.'

'Well, I hope you win.'

'So do I. Anyway, tour over, that's five pounds please.'

'A bargain,' said Sarah. 'I wish I had somewhere like this: somewhere to go, apart from my bedroom.'

'The only thing is,' I said, 'I'll have to get a heater in here. It's freezing . . .'

Suddenly Molly began to growl. Fierce growls which began deep in her throat.

'What is it, Molly?' I asked.

'She can probably hear the squirrels; they are often in our garden at night now,' said Sarah.

Molly's growling grew louder.

'It might be nothing,' I said. 'But Molly's a pretty good guard dog, you know. One night she started howling and wouldn't stop. Next morning Grandad discovered there'd been a burglary just down the road.'

'Shall I go and see then?' said Sarah.

'It's all right,' I said firmly. 'I'll go. You stay here with Molly.'

'Don't scare the squirrels, will you?' called Sarah after me. 'They're really such timid creatures you know.'

'It must be amazing knowing all about ghosts . . . and squirrels,' I muttered.

Outside the wind stung my cheeks. It had turned 'proper chilly' as Grandad would say. The wind sent the leaves scurrying across the grass. I was certain Molly had heard an animal in the garden. But I didn't think it was a squirrel.

Up at the top of our garden we get rats. They live next door in their compost heap. Then they creep over to our house at night. My mum's always complaining about them. But I like rats. They fascinate me.

I stood by our fence. I couldn't see a thing. But Molly was barking like crazy now. There must be something out here. I stared across at the garden. And that's when I saw something move. A shape. Only it was bigger than an animal. Much bigger.

Someone really was out here. A human. Was it Sarah? Had she wandered out of the shed to see what was going on? That would be just like her.

'Sarah,' I hissed.

The shape glided towards me. The face was shadowy and hard to see at first. It was the green I spotted. The green of my school uniform.

The ghost was here – in my back garden.

'What are you doing here?' I cried, my voice wobbling.

He didn't answer. He just kept oozing

towards me, his feet making no sound. Now I could see he was smiling. A terrible, hideous smile.

Then I heard him whisper my name. 'Alfie.' That made it even worse. I knew it was no accident he was in my garden. He had come looking for me. I should get away from him. But I couldn't move. I was rooted to the spot. It was as if he'd put me under some kind of spell.

I must get away. I knew I was in danger. 'Help.' But the word seemed to be trapped in my throat. 'Help,' I croaked again.

Out of nowhere came this loud bang. I jumped in the air. I thought it was a gun going off. Then something came charging towards me: a dark, furious shape. It ran right at me. I nearly fell over.

'What the . . . ?' I began. Then I started to laugh with relief and astonishment. 'Molly,' I cried. 'Did you hear me? Did you come out to

protect me?' I bent down beside her. Molly was panting and looking confused as if she couldn't quite believe what she'd done. For the ghost had gone, fading into the air like smoke. But my heart was still roaring inside my head.

Then I saw Sarah coming towards us. 'Isn't it wonderful!' she exclaimed. 'Molly was in the shed getting more and more worked up until she just leapt up, pushed open the shed door and flew outside. I wonder what made her do that?'

'It was me,' I said. 'Molly heard me calling for help.' I stood up.

For a second Sarah thought I was messing about. But then she realized I wasn't. Her voice tightened. 'Do you know what's out here, then?'

'Oh yes,' I said, grimly. 'And that's not such great news. It was that ghost, the one I saw in the padded cell.'

'What! So are you sure?' Suddenly she sounded frightened and anxious; Molly gave a low growl as if in sympathy.

'Of course I'm sure.' My voice rose. 'It was standing right in front of me.'

'But what's it doing here?'

'I was hoping you could tell me. You're the

one who's read fifty books about ghosts.' We were practically screaming at each other.

'Somehow that ghost's followed me home!' I cried. 'It even called me by name.'

'Oh no!' cried Sarah.

'What do you mean by that?'

'Nothing really, only . . . but no, that can't be true.'

I glared at her in mounting frustration. But there was no time to ask her anything else, as there were new voices in the garden.

'What are you shouting about?' demanded Mum, marching towards us. Grandad was with her.

But then Grandad spotted Molly. 'Here, girl,' he whispered. But I don't think he expected Molly to start moving towards him. But that is what she did. She didn't run or anything. Instead, she crept towards Grandad as if she was stalking a bird: very warily and slowly. But she was walking again with her new legs. It was just wonderful to see. Grandad was so chuffed he couldn't speak at first. Then he looked up at me. 'That's magic, that is,' he said. 'Well done, lad.'

'What did you do?' asked Mum.

I felt a right fraud. 'Oh, well, nothing really,

I got Molly to think I needed rescuing . . . and she forgot all about her fear.'

'Just magic,' repeated Grandad. 'There'll be no stopping her now, will there?' He rubbed Molly's head. 'I think we'll both be good for a few more years yet, eh girl?'

'You'd better be,' I said.

Mum invited Sarah to stay for tea. The four of us, and Molly, sat round the table – then Rachel came back from a friend's house.

Grandad and Molly did a special demonstration for Rachel. But Rachel just said, 'It's like she's moving in slow motion.' Rachel didn't understand at all.

Then Grandad invited Sarah and me round tomorrow for our tea. I never got a chance to ask Sarah any more about the ghost. I had a feeling she was avoiding me. But later that night she called.

'I'm sorry I wasn't much help tonight,' she

said. It was unusual for Sarah to apologize about anything. 'But I just want you to know I'm taking all my books on ghosts to bed with me. One of them must be able to explain how that ghost turned up in your garden tonight.'

'Earlier you started to tell me something.'

'Did I?' she said vaguely.

'You know you did.'

'Look, I'd rather not tell you any more until I've had a chance to do some more research.'

'Tell me now.'

'Well, I don't want to scare you.'

'Just spit it out.'

'All right. I think we might have been on the wrong track. I don't think that ghost is haunting the detention room – it's haunting you.'

'What!' I exclaimed.

'Now, I don't know for sure. But I think it's very strange you're the only one who ever sees it.'

'I don't want to keep seeing it. I'm quite happy for someone else to take a turn. Like you, for instance.'

'There's no need to be nasty. I'd be very interested in seeing that ghost. You know I would. But it never materializes for me . . . only to you.'

'So why is it haunting me?'

'That, I don't know . . . yet. But as soon as I work it out I'll give you a call.'

'How kind. Meanwhile this ghost could pop up at any time.'

'Yes, I suppose so.'

'Great – you've really cheered me up, haven't you? I'm sure I'll sleep better for knowing that. Thanks, Sarah.'

'You're the worst person ever. I don't know why I'm helping you.'

'Well, you haven't actually helped me,' I began.

At that Sarah rang off. I knew I'd been mean to her. It wasn't really her fault. I just had to take it out on someone. For I was becoming more and more confused – and scared. Something was going on here. Something bad. But I couldn't begin to understand it.

It took me ages to get to sleep. I'd jump awake thinking the ghost was in my room. Then I dreamt it had turned into a bat, swooping down on me out of the darkness. I even saw its fangs. I yelled and woke myself up.

What a relief. Except when I opened my eyes it was pitch dark. That really thick blackness, like a great fog. I hate waking up at this time. I tried to snuggle down into bed. I was just closing my eyes when I heard something.

Someone was calling me.

Years ago when I was in the bath one night this high, thin voice rose up out of the darkness calling, 'Alfie, Alfie.' I shook for the rest of the night. Later I discovered there was another, older Alfie who lived across the road from me. That voice was his mum calling him in to bed. I often heard her after that. But her voice still sounded strange and spooky. I was secretly very relieved when they moved away. And I never heard anyone else calling to me out of the darkness.

Until now.

It was a dream, the end of a dream. It had to be.

But then I heard it again.

'Alfie.'

It sounded nearer this time. If I opened my eyes would I see a figure in pale green uniform? Would he give me another of his terrible smiles?

What was he doing here? Why was he tormenting me like this? I should face up to him, tell him to leave me alone.

And in the daytime I could have done that. I'm not a total coward. But right then I was. I just buried my head under the covers whimpering slightly, like Molly. It was dark under there too. But it was a different kind of darkness. And it was very warm. I sank deeper and deeper into the warmth.

I stayed there until it was light. Then I peeped out. He'd gone. But I knew he'd be back. Sarah was right.

It wasn't the padded cell he was haunting: it was me.

CHAPTER NINE

Next day moved like a slug. I was dead tired
but Crumble kept asking me questions in
class. 'Glad you're still with us,' he said to me
in his sarky way. But my mind kept drifting
back to the ghost. The way he'd just suddenly
appeared in my garden. That horrible smile.

Where was he now? Would I look up and see
him staring in the window at me?

I didn't see him, but I had a horrible feeling
he wasn't far away.

I watched out for Sarah. I needed to talk to

her. But she wasn't at school. That seemed a bit strange. She'd been healthy enough last night.

After school I was going round to Grandad's for my tea. But I called in at Sarah's house first. I wondered what my friends would say if they could see me: calling for the Smurf.

Her mum answered the door. She had steely grey hair and looked nearly as old as Grandad. She smiled welcomingly at me.

'I just wondered if Sarah was all right?' I said.

'She's much better now thank you . . . She had one of her heads,' she added, as if I knew all about it. 'You're Alfie, aren't you?'

'That's right.'

'Well, come in, come in.'

Sarah was sitting at this large, old table. She was writing in her notebook. She looked surprised to see me.

Her mum treated me like royalty. 'Now sit down on the sofa in the corner there, Alfie,' said Sarah's mum. 'That's the most comfortable chair in here. Is that all right for you?'

'It's fine.'

'And would you like a glass of orange and a biscuit, Alfie?'

'Not just now, thanks.'

'Are you sure? Well you're most welcome. We worry it's rather lonely for Sarah here all the time without even a brother or sister to talk to, just us old-timers. And we don't bite, you know. In fact, we're very friendly.'

Sarah sat there squirming. And after her mum had gone she said, 'I'm really sorry about that.'

'That's OK; all parents are embarrassing, it's compulsory. Sorry, I was a bit snidey last night.'

'You'd had a shock.'

'That's true – how are you feeling?'

'I haven't been ill,' said Sarah briskly. 'I've been doing some research for you.'

'Oh, thanks . . . by the way, you might want to put this in your notebook: it turned up again.'

Sarah was staring intently at me now.

'Where?'

'In the middle of the night it started calling my name out.'

'And did you see it?'

'No, it was too dark.' I didn't add that I was hidden under the covers at the time.

Sarah sucked her pen thoughtfully. 'I don't understand why this ghost should fix on you of all people.'

'Oh, thanks.'

'I've been thinking about it all day. I've got some theories.'

'Go on.'

'He might be trying to get a message to you.'

'Well, why doesn't he just say his piece and go.'

Sarah shook her head.

'Besides, what could a ghost possibly have to say to me.'

'All right,' said Sarah sharply. 'It's only a theory. I've got another one.'

'Amaze me.'

'You see, some ghosts are what they call mischievous. They like playing little tricks on people. I suppose it must be quite frustrating being a ghost.'

'My heart bleeds for them . . . and so you

reckon he likes stirring things up for me and giving me a scare?'

'I think so – although I expect Molly gave him a bit of a scare last night.'

'Yeah, she was brilliant, so I should be safe around Grandad's house tonight anyway.'

'Oh, I don't think the ghost will come anywhere near you while Molly's about. Animals are very psychic, you know.' She got up. 'There's something else about this haunting . . . a kind of missing piece of the jigsaw. Once I've worked that out I'll have cracked the case. So leave it to me – I'm really good at solving puzzles.'

'But you're really good at everything, aren't you, Sarah?'

Sarah did a blinky double-take. 'I don't have to help you, you know.'

Next door Grandad was waiting for us. 'Come into the kitchen,' he said. Then he pointed out

of the window. Molly was in the garden. Most afternoons Grandad would carry Molly to her favourite spot and she'd lie there sleeping for hours. But today was different; today Molly was on her feet (or paws) sniffing everything in the garden.

'She's been round that garden three times while I've been watching her,' said Grandad.

'She's catching up with all the smells she's missed,' I said.

'Actually,' said Sarah, 'she's reclaiming her territory; all dogs do it.'

'Took her out for a walk today,' said Grandad. 'We just went up to the top of the road and back, but I must have been gone an hour. We kept being stopped. It's true, you know, you speak to a lot more people when you've got a dog.'

'She'll be giving her pawprint for autographs soon. She's a star, like me,' I said. 'Incidentally, Grandad, this is not exactly a hint or anything, but I'm starving.'

'Tell me something I don't know,' replied Grandad. 'We can start taking the food into the living room, but I thought we'd better wait for our other guest.'

'What other guest?' I demanded.

'Oh didn't I mention it?' said Grandad. 'We're being joined by an old friend of mine, a lady-friend, actually.'

'A lady-friend,' I echoed contemptuously. I hope this didn't mean Grandad was going to spend the evening staring dreamily into the eyes of some old trout, like those couples on coffee adverts.

'She's just a very old friend,' said Grandad. 'I hadn't seen her for years, but she's here visiting, so I invited her round for tea – that's all.' But his neck had turned bright red and he half-ran into the living room.

'You are mean,' hissed Sarah.

'What?'

'Didn't you notice your grandad was all dressed up in his smart brown jacket.'

'I didn't, actually.'

'Well he obviously likes her, and why shouldn't he have a friend in his twilight years?'

'Because he's got me – and Molly – and even you, I suppose. And that's plenty.'

Grandad appeared out of the living room. 'Come on, you two, stop gassing. Put some food out.'

In the kitchen Grandad started piling these sandwiches on to a plate. The pile grew higher and higher until it looked like a skyscraper.

'Who is this woman who's coming round, Grandad?'

'She's called Mrs Porter.'

I considered. 'Mrs Porter. I've heard that name.'

Grandad shook his head. 'No, you wouldn't know her. You see . . .' At that moment the doorbell rang.

'Ah, that must be her,' said Grandad.

'Not necessarily,' I replied. 'It could be Father Christmas calling early.'

'I'll give you Father Christmas,' muttered Grandad.

A moment later I heard a woman's voice say, 'I'm not too early, am I?' and Grandad say, 'No, of course not.' They went into the living room. He introduced her to Sarah, while I hovered uncertainly in the doorway. I hate meeting people for the first time. Finally, I took a deep

breath and joined them.

Mrs Porter had her back to me. She was talking to Sarah. But Grandad spotted me. 'And this is my illustrious grandson, Alfie.'

Mrs Porter turned round. A large woman in a green suit. She was smiling. Then she wasn't. And instead, she gave me this really funny look, as if I'd just dropped hot jam down her neck.

She let out this gasp, swayed a bit, then Grandad sprang forward and helped her on to the sofa. He knelt beside her, while Sarah opened a window.

'Oh dear,' cried Mrs Porter, 'I'm sorry about that.'

'Don't worry, you probably got too hot,' said Sarah. But I knew that wasn't what had happened.

I knew it was me.

One look at yours truly was enough to send

that woman spinning off into darkness.

I'd shocked her, terrified her.

And then I remembered something. That day in the padded cell, he'd spoken about Mrs Porter.

The ghost.

Was this something to do with him too? Had he somehow wormed his way in here? Was nowhere safe from him?

Mrs Porter smiled apologetically at Grandad. 'I thought I was going to pass out then.' Grandad told her not to worry; it was a humid evening. Sarah started fussing about with the cushions.

I didn't move. I felt oddly guilty. Then she sat up. She saw me. For a moment that look of terror returned. Her hand actually jerked.

After which she tried to recover herself. 'I'm sorry . . . It's . . .' She seemed to be searching for words. 'It's just uncanny,' she whispered, at last.

Then she tried smiling at me. And that made it even more eerie. Grandad was bewildered. He thought she was rambling. He said she needed a sugary drink. But Sarah kept looking across at me, her eyes nearly as wide as Mrs Porter's.

Propped up on her cushions Mrs Porter started to talk. 'You look exactly like an ex-pupil of mine.' She spoke very slowly, as if she'd just woken up from a heavy sleep. 'He was such a brilliant pupil. Yet he was also painfully shy, poor lad . . .'

'He's dead now, isn't he?' I interrupted.

'Yes, I'm afraid so.' Her voice fell away. 'It was very sudden. A dreadful shock.'

'And was he called Alfred?' asked Sarah.

'Why, yes, dear. Alfred Goddard. However did you know that?'

'Just a lucky guess,' murmured Sarah.

'And did he die at the school?' I asked suddenly.

Mrs Porter looked taken aback by the question. 'At school – why, no, he didn't.'

'But he looked a bit like young Alfie, here?' said Grandad.

'He's the spitting image of him,' said Mrs Porter.

'Oh no, he isn't,' I said. 'I'm much better looking for a start.'

'Listen to him,' said Grandad. 'You'd think he'd seen this boy. I'm afraid he was a bit before Alfie's time, wasn't he?'

'Oh yes, he must have died twenty . . . no, nearer thirty years ago.' She gave a funny little laugh. 'I must admit, when I first saw Alfie here, I thought he was a ghost.'

Grandad laughed too. 'First and last time you've ever been mistaken for a ghost, eh Alfie?'

I smiled grimly.

Then from outside came a loud, indignant bark from Molly. 'Poor old Molly's feeling all left out,' said Grandad. 'I must bring her in for you.' But Mrs Porter asked Grandad not to let Molly get too near as she was very nervous of dogs.

'She won't hurt you,' said Grandad.

'They all say that.' replied Mrs Porter. Grandad's smile slipped away. I had a feeling he wouldn't be inviting Mrs Porter round again for a while. Alfred wasn't mentioned any more. Although every so often I'd catch Mrs Porter giving me these 'looks' as if she couldn't believe I was real. I think she still found me a bit spooky.

Afterwards Sarah and I stood chatting outside her house.

'I don't know. First of all, you see a ghost. Now you're mistaken for one,' said Sarah lightly.

'Yeah, it's been quite a week,' I replied, equally lightly. 'I bet that Mrs Porter will dream about me tonight.'

'Poor woman,' said Sarah. 'I hadn't realized you looked so much like this Alfred.'

'I don't, really.'

'Are you sure?'

'I have met the geezer. And I'll probably see him again tonight: no doubt he'll have some more late-night entertainment for me.' The smile froze on my lips. 'I nearly asked Grandad if I could borrow Molly tonight, you know.'

'You should have done.'

'Nah. My mum would go mad for a start. She didn't like me keeping hamsters in my bedroom. She thinks pets should be kept outside – they're unhygienic, all that rubbish. So it'll just be me and the ghost again tonight. How long do you think he'll stick around?'

'I'm not sure,' said Sarah. 'Look, I am still investigating this case and I'm sure I'm going to make a breakthrough really soon.'

The following evening I'd just finished my tea when Sarah rang up. 'Did you see the ghost last night?'

'No, I was dead to everything. I didn't wake up once. So maybe he was calling to me but I never heard him – you were away from school again.'

'Was I? Well, I never knew that.'

'Hey, I'm the sarky one.'

'But listen to this,' said Sarah. 'I've cracked the case.'

'What.'

'Yes, I've worked it all out.'

'So tell me, tell me.'

'Well I'm not sure you're going to like it.'

'Why?'

'Look, I think it's best if I come round.'

'All right, sure – but why can't you tell me over the phone?'

But Sarah had already rung off.

CHAPTER TEN

I told Mum Sarah was coming round. Mum
looked pleased. 'She's a nice girl, isn't she?'

'Not particularly,' I replied. 'But I've got to
discuss something with her. We'll be in the old
shed.'

Mum brought out a fan heater and a bean
bag for Sarah to sit on.

I went back inside. I was getting impatient.
Then I saw Sarah in our little porch. I saw her
through the pebbled glass on the front door. I
pulled open the door just as her hand touched

the doorbell. She jumped back in surprise. I love doing that to people.

Inside the shed I switched on the heater. It whirred away. I was glad Mum had brought it. It was really cold in here tonight. Sarah sat on the bean bag. She was wearing a sports jumper and jeans. She dressed better out of school. She was also wearing these Kickers lookalikes. But they weren't real Kickers. I can always tell. I was sprawled out by the door. I made some silly comments – as I usually do – but my throat felt dry.

Sarah stared down at her notebook. 'I wanted to find out more about your ghost. Now we know his name was Alfred Goddard.' She sounded as if she were reading out her homework in class. 'Mrs Porter said he died nearly thirty years ago. So I thought there must have been something in our local paper about him – and his accident. And they keep all the local

papers at the library, don't they?'

I gave her a 'get on with it' nod.

'Now I know the librarian, and she was very helpful. We went through all these old papers and discovered Mrs Porter was wrong. Alfred Goddard didn't die nearly thirty years ago. He died *exactly* thirty years ago.' Then with something of a flourish she unfolded a piece of paper from the back of her notebook. 'I made this copy for you.'

I stretched across and took the photocopy. There was a headline: 'TEN-YEAR-OLD BOY DIES IN CYCLING ACCIDENT' and a photograph. The picture was smudged but I recognized the boy all right.

'As soon as I saw the face I knew why Mrs Porter was so upset,' said Sarah.

'What do you mean?'

'He could be your double.'

'Sarah, if you want to live you'll stop saying that.'

'Why?'

'I should think that's obvious.'

'Not to me.'

'All right, for a start he's about as ugly as Quasimodo.'

'Don't be silly.'

'And look at his hair. It's like a mop. Turn him upside down and you can wipe the kitchen floor with that hair.'

'All right.'

'He's just a total geek. Something no-one's ever called me.'

'You're lucky,' said Sarah quietly. 'Look, calm down; his personality is obviously totally different to yours, except for one thing: you both love cycling. In fact, that was how he died, you know. He was out on his bike when he collided with this lorry.'

'I'm not really interested.'

'But you have to know one thing for your own safety.'

I looked across at her: 'What are you talking about?'

'Alfred Goddard died on October 29th 1967: that's thirty years ago next week.'

I shrugged my shoulders.

'But that's the day you're in the cycling race.'

That did give me a jolt. I'll admit that. But I quickly recovered. 'So what.'

'Well maybe it's nothing,' said Sarah, ' but it's a very strange coincidence, isn't it?' She leaned forward. 'I think it's best you pull out of the race.'

'You're joking.'

'Not at all.'

I shook my head in amazement. 'I don't believe you. I've been practising for this race for weeks. I've collected all the sponsorship money.'

'I know that,' said Sarah. 'But listen, there's something else I've got to tell you.'

'I can't wait.'

'I've been doing some reading about this, and what happens when you see a ghostly apparition who's your double – or time-twin, that's the proper term for it. So Alfred is your time-twin.'

'No, he's not,' I muttered through clenched teeth, 'because he's not my double.'

Sarah ignored this. 'Well usually the time-twin brings chaos with it. There was this story of a teacher who was sitting at her desk when all the pupils burst out laughing because they could see her time-twin out in the playground. The teacher ran up and down the playground but she never caught her double. And this kept happening until, in the end, the teacher got the sack. She – or rather her time-twin – was just too much trouble. But,' Sarah leaned forward, 'she was one of the lucky ones. Usually when people see their time-twin they meet their doom shortly afterwards.'

'You mean they snuff it?'

'Yes. And I'm not saying this to worry you. But if I didn't tell you and then something bad happened I'd feel dreadful.'

'I don't think I'd feel too good either. So I'm doomed, am I?'

'Well, you might be. Yes . . . sorry.'

I tried to laugh. But my breath caught somewhere in my throat. For a moment the only sound was the heater whirring away: it was a noisy heater, but totally useless. For the shed was still freezing cold.

I didn't want to stay here another second. And I didn't want to hear any more of Sarah's fanciful nonsense either.

I stumbled to my feet.

'What you're forgetting, Sarah, is that I don't think this ghost is my double. I bet there are hundreds of people who look more like me than him, probably hundreds of ghosts too.' Sarah stared up at me, surprised by my outburst. 'Anyway, if we stay here any longer we'll both be covered in frost. So shall we go?'

Now Sarah looked even more surprised.

'And I don't want this, thanks.' I thrust the photocopy back at her. She took the photograph from me, then gasped. It fell out of her hands.

I looked at her. 'What's going on?' I asked quietly.

Her voice was even lower. I could hardly hear her. 'I was just going to ask you to switch the heater off . . . it's boiling hot.'

A shudder ran through me. 'But it's like the Arctic in here.'

'No it isn't, Alfie,' whispered Sarah, urgently.

Suddenly she got to her feet. She walked over to me. She stood very still. Then she said softly: 'It even smells colder around you.'

'All right, all right,' I snapped. 'Don't make a big deal of it. I've just been standing in a draft.' I dashed over to where Sarah had been sitting. 'I'll soon warm up now.' I stood there, willing myself to get warmer.

Sarah didn't move at all. She looked like a figure in a wax museum. 'Feel any warmer?' she asked anxiously at last.

'Yeah, a bit,' I muttered. But I didn't. None of the heat was reaching me. It was as if there was an invisible wall of cold all around me. And nothing could get through it.

I couldn't fib any more. 'I can't get warm, Sarah.'

'Oh,' said Sarah, but it was more like a cry.

'I feel like someone's dropping ice down my back. Freezing cold ice.'

'Actually, ice can only be cold, otherwise . . .' The expression on my face made Sarah shut up.

'Well don't just stand there like a frozen robin,' I cried. 'Do something.'

'Yes, yes, of course. Just tell me what to do and I'll do it.'

'I don't know what to do – I don't know.' My voice was starting to shake all over the place. 'Sarah, what's happening to me?'

She took a deep breath. 'Well, don't panic or anything, but I think he's here. Your ghost.'

'Don't call him my ghost!' I practically screamed.

'Sorry, sorry. But it's him anyway.'

'Oh great – great. What's he doing this for anyway? What is he . . . ?' But I couldn't say any more. The words died on my lips. For my trophy had suddenly come to life. It was jumping about my shelf like a clockwork toy that had just been wound up. Then it shot right up into the air.

Sarah sprang back in horror as it whizzed around the shed. I pressed my feet hard on to the floor. I had the weirdest sensation that any second I might float off too. I swayed slightly, while unseen hands started tugging away at my magazines. The magazines twitched and shook and then they were flapping above our heads like giant bats.

Then I heard a strange, whimpering noise. That was me. I was scared out of my wits. Sarah grabbed hold of my sleeve. She didn't need to say a word.

We fled.

We ran – me skidding in my haste – into the house. We fell gasping into the kitchen.

'Alfie, have you got my hair-dryer?'

I looked up to see my sister staring accusingly at me. If she loses something she always goes, 'Alfie, have you got it?' She'll keep on asking me as well. Normally it really annoys me and I decide I will take something of hers just to get my own back. But tonight it was almost a relief; it seemed to bring everything back to normal.

'What would I want with your hair-dryer?'

'Well if I find it in your room,' said Rachel, 'I'm going to tell Mum.' She gave me one of her long looks. But she didn't ask why Sarah and I were out of breath. Perhaps she didn't even notice.

Then she flounced off.

I paced up and down. I was still shivering. But I was getting warmer – at last.

'I think he's gone,' I said.

'Good,' cried Sarah so firmly I couldn't help teasing her.

'I thought you were the one who wanted to see ghosts – it was one of your ambitions.'

'Not ones like him who just act silly.'

At once I was angry again. 'He's got no right to keep bothering me, has he? It's like he's stalking me.'

Sarah looked up. 'The Ghost Stalker – I suppose I ought to write this up while it's still fresh in my mind.'

'I don't think we'll ever forget what happened tonight.'

'That's true.' Sarah dug in her pocket for her notebook. It wasn't there. 'I must have left it in the shed. Oh, well, I can always pick it up another time.'

I nodded in agreement. But then I said, 'What are we saying? That's my shed. And no poxy ghost is keeping me out of there. I'll get it now.'

'Are you sure?'

'Yes,' I said as confidently as I could. I felt brave and scared, bits of each.

'Well, I'll come with you,' said Sarah.

'OK, let's do it fast then,' I said. 'I think it's best not to think about things sometimes, just do them.'

We half-ran to the shed. The door was already open. I strode inside, the way teachers do when they think someone has done something wrong. The heater was still whirring away.

'It's like a sauna in here,' I said. Sarah and I exchanged relieved glances. Then I saw what he'd done to my shed. My cycling trophy lay on its side in the corner, while my magazines were strewn all over the place. My mum would go mad if she thought I'd left the shed like this.

'Look at the mess he's made,' I said. We both started piling up the cycling magazines again. 'And I had them in order too. It'll take me ages to sort them out now.'

'It's just so stupid of him to do this,' said Sarah. 'I don't understand him, especially as Mrs Porter said he was such a nice, quiet boy.'

'Being dead has certainly changed his personality for the worse,' I said.

'Maybe he's jealous of you.'

'Hmm.' I rather liked the idea.

'I mean, I think it's quite significant that it was your cycling trophy and magazines that he threw about.'

'You could be right. Well he won't be winning any more trophies now.' For a moment I felt quite triumphant. But then I added, 'Still, he'll be back, won't he?'

'I'm sure he will.'

'He probably really enjoys scaring me, makes him feel all powerful when really . . .' I stopped.

Sarah gave me a puzzled look. 'What?'

'You said ghosts haven't got any reflection, didn't you?'

'That's right.'

'So actually they're nothing. Ghosts are just

shadows aren't they? Nothing else. And they can't do anything to you, can they? All right, they can make the atmosphere turn cold and throw a few things about – but that's all, isn't it? That's why ghosts are always creeping about at night when you're on your own. I mean, my ghost won't slip into a chair when I'm with Mum or Rachel, will he?'

'What are you getting at?' asked Sarah.

'I'm saying that ghosts are just an illusion really. In a crowd in daylight they wouldn't be any scarier than a moth. That's why they pick their moments and they know that.' I paused. 'They know that fear always feeds upon itself.'

'Where did you read that?'

'I don't know, but it's quite good, isn't it?' I got up. 'Look, Sarah, next time that ghost appears I'll be ready for him.'

Sarah's eyes grew wide. 'What do you mean?'

I hesitated. 'I don't know. I'll challenge him to an arm wrestle or something.'

'What?'

'I'll show him he can't scare me. Then he'll fly off and find some other poor person to bother.'

Sarah looked doubtful. 'I don't think you should do anything until I'm here. After all, as far as ghosts are concerned you are a total amateur . . .'

'But if I don't do something, Sarah, this haunting could go on for weeks . . . even years.'

'But you mustn't challenge the ghost or do anything until I'm here,' she said, staring intently at me.

'Why?'

'It could be very dangerous – for you. Now promise me you won't do anything.'

'All right, Sarah, I promise,' I said.

But I crossed my fingers when I said it.

CHAPTER ELEVEN

That night I woke up, freezing. My duvet must have slipped off again. It was always doing that. I stretched my hand out. The duvet was there. It hadn't moved.

Then I knew.

My enemy was back.

My heart went thump, thump, thump. I tried to steady myself by making out all the familiar shapes in my room. There was my desk with my little television on top of it, above that I could see my model aeroplanes. Next there was my little wooden chair.

My heart stopped.

There was someone sitting on that chair. I could see him. A dark silhouette. Then I remembered. I must have slung my clothes over the chair. I must have been tired. Those clothes had caught me out before. But not this time.

'Alfie.' That voice again. It sounded very near. Where was he?

I swallowed hard. I mustn't let him scare me. Otherwise he'd win again.

'Yeah, what do you want?' I called back. My voice sounded thin and scratchy. But it began to gather power as I went on. 'You think you're scaring me but you're not. I've coughed up scarier things than you.'

I began to laugh contemptuously. My heart was pounding furiously. Sarah had said I mustn't challenge him. But I had no choice. You've got to stand up to bullies. And that's all he was.

'Come on then, show yourself. Stop hiding in the shadows,' I demanded. As soon as I switch on the light you'll disappear into whatever darkness you've come from. Well I'm going to put the light on right now. So prepare to vanish.'

I stumbled out of bed. My legs felt very wobbly, as if I'd been ill in bed for days. But I was determined. I walked over to the switch. Then I stopped. And my whole body shook, as a memory rushed through me.

I'd hung my clothes up in the wardrobe tonight. Mum had come in and insisted. She said it stopped the clothes from smelling stale. She said . . . never mind what she said.

There was someone sitting on my chair.

The shape stirred. I saw the green uniform. I saw the pale white face. I heard him say, *'Danger.'* Only his voice sounded really close now, as if he was whispering the word in my ear.

'Danger.' He said it again. He was taunting me, mocking me.

That's when something in me snapped. I leaped forward and swung a punch at him. I punched him smack on the face.

And my hand didn't go through him. I

touched something solid, and icy cold.

I pulled my hand back. It stung a little. I was staring into emptiness. I started yelling. 'And if you come back I'll punch you again. Have you got that? You're not wanted here . . .'

I switched the light on. Then I started in horror. In the mirror was a horrible face, all twisted with anger and fear.

It was my face, and it scared me. It didn't look like me. I switched the light off again, scrambled into bed, pulling the cold sheets around me. I felt ashamed of myself for getting so mad. I'd done something wrong tonight and I had a feeling I would pay dearly for it.

But in the morning I felt differently. I'd had to attack the ghost. He was a monster. He'd left me no choice.

Now he'd gone into the darkness, never to be seen again.

It was all over.

I'd defeated him.

CHAPTER TWELVE

Next day I told Sarah what had happened.

It was Friday afternoon and we were taking Molly for a walk. Each day she managed to go a little further.

'No sign of the ghost yet?' asked Sarah. Then she answered her own question. 'He might wait a while before he returns again.'

'Actually, I saw the ghost last night,' I replied, enjoying the look of amazement on Sarah's face.

Then I told her what had happened. We

stopped walking. We stood at the top of Grandad's road. Sarah didn't say a word. She was listening really intently. I could hear her breathing. Then I told her about me punching the ghost, and she sighed loudly.

'You promised you wouldn't do anything until I was there,' she said.

'I know.' I nearly added that I'd crossed my fingers at the time, but I didn't.

'And you shouldn't have punched him. That's so typical of a boy. Now you've just got him mad. He won't give you a minute's peace.'

'Won't he?'

'No. You'll probably find he keeps switching things on and off in your room tonight. Like lights and televisions . . . anything electrical. Ghosts often do that when they're really angry.'

I tried to look as if I wasn't too bothered. 'I'll just switch the telly back on and punch him in the face again.'

'No, you mustn't do that,' cried Sarah in such a high voice that Molly obviously thought Sarah was talking to her and started barking excitedly. Sarah bent down and let Molly lick her ear. 'I really wish I wasn't going off,' she said.

'You smell all right to me.'

Sarah didn't even pretend to smile. She had to go away with her parents for the weekend. 'Now you mustn't do anything else to antagonize the ghost. Just wait until I get back. Do you understand?' She sounded like a teacher speaking to a particularly dense pupil. Then she started scribbling in her notebook. She tore out a page. 'Here's the phone number of where I'll be. Ring me anytime.' Sarah said she would be back by five o'clock on Sunday. I promised to go round and give her a full report.

And at five o'clock on Sunday she was waiting outside her house for me.

'My parents are prowling about,' she said, 'so I thought it might be easier if we talked out here.' We sat on her wall. She looked a bit tense. But I had good news for her. Nothing had happened. He didn't whisper my name, sit in my chair, move anything about – or switch on my television.

'I really think he's gone,' I said, finally.

Sarah didn't look as pleased as I'd expected. In fact she almost seemed disappointed. 'He could still come back,' she said.

'I don't think so.' I couldn't resist adding, 'I scared him off. I gave him quite a hard punch, you know. He knows I won't take any more of his nonsense, so he's slunk off. I wish he'd told me where my jacket was, but otherwise I feel pretty pleased with myself. I can get on with the important things – like training for the cycling race.'

A look of horror crossed Sarah's face. 'You're not still doing that?'

'Yeah, why not?'

'But you can't!' exclaimed Sarah. 'You are in danger on that day.'

Now Sarah was starting up all this rubbish about me being in danger. She went on. 'Your time-twin met his doom in a cycling race exactly thirty years ago – everything points to it happening again.'

'For the eight millionth time,' I said, 'he's not my time-twin. And he's gone now.'

'We don't know he's gone for good.'

'I do,' I replied firmly.

'Maybe he's waiting until the day of the race and then he'll suddenly jump out and then you'll lose your balance and go hurtling off your bike . . .'

I jumped up. 'I'm not listening to any more of this.'

'All right then,' said Sarah. 'Do what you like. Go off and meet your doom. But I'm not helping you any more.'

'You didn't help much anyway,' I snapped. 'You might have read all the books, but it was me who got rid of the ghost. Not you.'

She didn't say another word, just stormed off back to her house. I heard her slam the door. I didn't go round to see Grandad and Molly as I'd planned. Instead, I set off on my bike. I cycled around for hours.

Over the next days Sarah and I never spoke. It was a bit petty, I know, but I was still very annoyed with her. She wasn't in charge of me. She couldn't tell me what to do. She didn't know everything.

We took Molly for walks separately and I tried to visit Grandad when she wasn't there.

Grandad noticed something was wrong. I knew he would. I was brushing Molly – I brush her every day – when Grandad said, 'What's up?'

I pretended I didn't know what he was talking about.

'You and young Sarah. Have you fallen out?'

I shrugged my shoulders. I didn't want to talk about it, even with Grandad. But he kept on staring at me, just like Molly does when she wants something.

'I don't know what's wrong.' I shrugged again. 'And I'm not bothered.'

'Of course you are,' said Grandad. 'She's your friend, isn't she?'

I should have said of course she isn't. No-one likes her. She's the Smurf. But I didn't say any of that. I didn't say anything at all.

'Good friends are worth keeping,' said Grandad. But then he changed the subject.

That's one thing about Grandad – he doesn't go on and on about things. He would be seeing

me off at the cycle race on Saturday. He and
Molly. Mum couldn't make it as she and
Rachel were going to my cousin's wedding.
They'd wanted me to go too – as a pageboy.
That's the sort of thing you do when you're
about two months old. I was far, far too old.
Even if I hadn't been in the race I'd have
missed the wedding after hearing that.

The night before the race Sarah spoke to me:
the first time for five days. We were in
Grandad's kitchen. I was at the sink filling up
Molly's bowl with water.

'Are you still going through with the race,
then?' she asked my back.

I whirled round. I was amazed by the question. 'Of course I am.' She immediately started
walking away. 'Look, Sarah, if I pull out then
the ghost's still beaten me, hasn't he?' I called
after her, 'Sarah, wait.'

But she just went on walking away.

Still, tomorrow when I walk in here, as right as rain, she'll have to say something then.

I'd settle for, 'Sorry, Alfie, you were completely right, as always.'

CHAPTER THIRTEEN

And then it was the day of the bike race. I woke up early. I lay in bed listening to the rain pattering against the window.

I could hear Mum and Rachel talking. They were in Rachel's bedroom. Mum's voice was low and reassuring. Rachel was getting in a flap about this wedding. I knew she would. She gets in a flap about everything. If she loses her hairbrush it's a major catastrophe.

Unlike me. This was the day I was supposed to meet my doom, yet I was calm. Sort of. I stomped into the bathroom. I started whistling. 'Stop making that terrible noise,' called my sister. 'You're giving me a headache.'

I whistled even louder. Downstairs Mum was cooking us a 'proper breakfast' – kippers. I started eating. But I wasn't as hungry as I'd expected.

Then from upstairs came a terrible wail. Mum rushed to the bottom of the stairs. 'Whatever's happened?'

'Nothing, except I can't go to the wedding,' cried Rachel.

'Why ever not?'

'I thought I'd mix up my pink glittery and my purple glittery nail polish and make my own colour but it's all gone wrong, and . . ..' her voice became positively tragic, 'I've run out of nail polish remover.'

'Don't panic,' said Mum, 'I'm sure I've got some, somewhere.' She tore upstairs while I went on picking at my kipper.

A short while later I heard them come downstairs again. 'Problem solved,' said Mum, breezing back into the kitchen.

I didn't look up. I didn't want to see my sister. Smelling her was bad enough.

'What a pong,' I said. 'You stink of nail polish.'

'Don't be silly,' said Mum briskly. 'Now, Rachel, you've got to eat something before we go to the hairdresser's. I insist. And – oh Alfie – you must be giving that kipper an inferiority complex. You've hardly touched it.'

'Yes I have,' I lied.

'Not nervous about this race, are you?'

'Of course not.'

'I'm sorry to miss seeing you off.'

'Don't worry about it.'

Mum smiled at me. 'But I'm looking forward to hearing all about it – and that reminds me – Rachel's staying on for the disco but I should be back by four o'clock at the latest, but just in case I'm delayed here's a key. Look after it, as it's my only spare . . .'

'Mum, what are you doing?' interrupted Rachel. 'You know he'll lose it.'

'No I won't,' I hissed fiercely. 'I never lose things.'

'What about your new jacket then?' she said. 'You lost that a while ago.'

'Oh go eat your nail polish,' I muttered.

Her voice rose. 'Honestly, Mum, if he loses that key we'll have to change all the locks and we just can't afford to do that.'

I gave her one of my filthiest stares then beamed at Mum. 'You know you can trust me.'

'Yes, I'm sure I can,' said Mum. She handed me the front doorkey to the accompaniment of much head shaking from Rachel. I liked having it. I should always have a key, really.

It was still drizzling with rain when I set off on my mountain bike. Dad had paid for it. I'd chosen this bike because of its colour – red (Manchester United's colour). Only everyone – and especially Mike – went on and on about how my bike was more pink than red. In the end they turned against the colour. I borrowed Grandad's Stanley knife and peeled off all the red (or pink) on the brake cables. It came off quite easily. Unfortunately there was mainly rust underneath. My mum went mad when she saw what I'd done. But I decided I'd made my bike look more individual.

We were meeting at the church. There was a big banner over the gate. Masses of people were there already including just about everyone from my form, and Crumble. I pretended not to see him. This was a Saturday. He was nothing to do with me today. Mike rode over to me. 'I got my new mountain bike,' he said. 'What do you think?'

'It looks pretty safe.'

'It is.' He went on boasting about how many gears it had. Then he laughed. 'You might at least paint yours. At the moment it's just like the skeleton of a bike.' Mike must have seen my face change for he started to backtrack. 'Still it's certainly different, I suppose.'

But I wasn't insulted. I just wish he hadn't used the word skeleton. Not today.

'Anyway, I've got some mates saving me a place in the front row,' said Mike. 'See you.' I was glad to see him go. He was annoying me.

I spotted Grandad with Molly. There was a

small crowd around them – or rather Molly. When she saw me Molly yelped excitedly. Grandad wished me luck. Then he exclaimed, 'I don't believe it!'

'What?'

He pointed. I didn't believe it either.

Sarah was wobbling towards us on what was undoubtedly the most awful bike I'd ever seen in my life. It even – and you won't believe this – had a basket at the front.

'This is a surprise,' declared Grandad.

Sarah couldn't reply at first; she was so out of breath. Riding that bike was probably the most exercise she'd had for years.

'What are you doing here?' I demanded.

'I've a perfect right to be here,' she snapped.

'Yes, but your bike – is it your mum's or your gran's?' Already people were sniggering at her. Even one or two of the parents were having a discreet chuckle. 'You've made a right show of yourself,' I said. Sarah just ignored me and bent down to pat Molly.

The vicar started nattering through a megaphone, so Grandad and Molly wished us luck again and then they joined the other onlookers at the side. But I went on questioning Sarah. 'You hate cycling. You told me that. So come

on, what's going on?'

'Mind your own business.'

'And what have you got in that basket, your mum's vegetables?'

I peered down to take a closer look. I saw a small green box with a red cross on it.

'A first-aid kit,' I exclaimed. 'But what . . . ?' I didn't need to say any more. Sarah had gone bright red. 'Is that for my benefit?' I demanded.

She didn't answer, just hunched her shoulders up.

'You're trying to wind me up, aren't you?'

'Look, just ignore me,' she said. 'Act as if I'm not here.'

'Don't worry, I will.'

I turned and faced the vicar who was introducing the stewards now: six guys in yellow jackets, who we'd see along the route to Westlake Park. The vicar was droning on about how one of the stewards had to sign our sponsorship form. I stopped listening. I looked again at Sarah. She really believed something bad was going to happen to me.

She had no right thinking that, unnerving me. I'd been doing all right until she'd appeared.

I sat on my bike lost in my own anger until I noticed something was happening. The race had started.

Mike was already way out of sight. So were half the other cyclists.

I shrugged my shoulders.

'I'm only here for a good laugh,' I announced to no-one in particular.

I decided to just try and enjoy myself. At least I know the route to Westlake Park well. More cyclists whizzed past me. I felt a bit lonely to tell the truth.

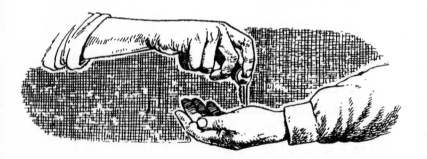

I wondered where Sarah was. Not that I wanted to talk to her. I stared around. I couldn't see her at all at first. Then I saw her, way, way at the back. She had both hands clasped on to the handlebars. She looked so uncomfortable I laughed out loud.

Then she started swerving about. She was going far too close to the kerb. She'd fall off that bike if she wasn't careful. Then she'd need the first-aid kit, not me.

I laughed again, then called out, 'Come out a bit more and try and keep in a straight line.'

She puffed towards me. Her eyes had gone all glassy. 'Don't worry about me; you go off and win the race.'

'No chance now,' I said.

'Are you blaming me?' she demanded.

'To be honest, I think me winning that trophy was a bit of a freak. Most of those cyclists are miles better than me.'

'Oh.' Her voice was a bit gentler. 'Well, goodbye then.'

She wobbled off. I followed her. She came to a corner. 'Put your hand out – signal you're going left.' I put my hand out but Sarah's never left the handlebars. 'What are you doing – why didn't you signal?' I cried.

'Well, I thought I'd leave signalling for today.'

'You can't leave it,' I spluttered. 'I can see I'm going to have to watch you.'

'Don't be silly,' she replied. But from then on we cycled together. We didn't say much, though. Then we passed one of the stewards: 'Frizzle Wood just ahead,' he said. 'Keep going'.

'Now Frizzle Wood, that's great,' I said. 'I often cycle through there.' I turned into a tour guide pointing out that it stretched on for two miles and took us out near the park. I started pointing out interesting things: 'That oak tree over there,' I said, 'is the biggest tree in Frizzle Wood.' I glanced idly at one of its branches.

I couldn't believe what I saw. My bike screeched to a halt.

Sarah ran straight into me.

'You shouldn't have stopped like that,' she exclaimed. 'Even I know that.'

It took a few moments to find my voice. Finally, in a kind of daze I turned round. 'Sarah, hanging from that branch over there . . . is a hand.'

CHAPTER FOURTEEN

Sarah's mouth opened and closed faster than any goldfish's.

'What did you say?'

'Look!' I couldn't stop trembling but she saw where I was pointing all right. On one of the bottom branches a hand was swinging gently in the breeze.

'But what's it doing there?' gasped Sarah.

'Well it's not growing there, that's for sure . . . his other hand is probably somewhere nearby. In fact, there'll be bits of him scattered all over this wood.'

'Ugh, don't. Anyway, how do you know it's a man's hand? It could be a woman's.'

'We've wandered into something very serious. We'd better go and tell someone — now.'

To be honest I didn't want to stay here another second. This wood was suddenly full of danger. The madman who'd done this could jump out at us at any second, eager to add our hands to his collection.

It was in this wood I'd meet my doom. That idea just popped into my head. I couldn't get it to leave.

I was all set to make a sharp exit when, to my amazement, Sarah got down off her bike. She scrambled past me.

'Sarah, what are you . . . ?' I began. Then, with a thud of horror I realized what she was going to do. 'Don't touch the dead man's hand!' I yelled. 'That's evidence.' I leapt off my bike and promptly tripped over. It wasn't my fault. This old tree root or whatever it was got in my way. I scrambled to my feet, trying to look as if I'd meant to do that. Anyway, I was too late; she had pulled the hand down from the branch. She was actually touching it.

I gaped at her in horror.

'Would you like me to perform a magic trick?' she asked.

It's the shock, I thought. It's turned her brain.

'With one swish, Alfie, I can turn the dead man's hand into a . . . Marigold.'

Moments later I was staring down at a pink washing-up glove and feeling distinctly stupid. 'You must admit, from a distance and turned inside out . . . well, even Your Majesty was fooled at first.'

'Only for a micro-second,' said Sarah. 'You see, I used my superior brain power.'

'Just a shame your superior brain power doesn't make you a better cyclist, isn't it?'

Sarah threw the Marigold at me. 'I thought you might want to keep it as evidence.'

'You're so funny.' I said. 'We used to blow these gloves up, you know, to make them look like cows' udders.'

'Yes, I could imagine you doing that,' replied Sarah. But she didn't say it in her usual looking-down-her-nose-at-you way.

I hung the Marigold back on the branch. 'I'll leave it here to scare someone else. And I bet it will, too. Come on then, we must go. We're supposed to be in a race. I wonder if we're last.'

We were. In fact, we reached the park just as the vicar was handing out the trophies. He'd already presented the first and second prizes. He was giving the third prize to Michael, of all people.

I made a face as if I'd just swallowed something very bitter. Sarah saw me. 'If it hadn't been for me you'd have been up there with the winners,' she said. I knew that wasn't true, but I nodded in agreement anyway.

A little group started clapping Sarah and me. Only they were clapping really slowly. Others joined in.

'They're all mocking us,' whispered Sarah. 'I hate them.'

'Stay cool and don't let them see you're upset,' I whispered back. 'Just act as if you're lapping it up.'

I put a big smile on my face, called out, 'Cheers, lads,' and waved at everyone. To my surprise, Sarah gave out some pretty regal waves too.

Afterwards I said loudly to the vicar, 'We figured if we couldn't come first we'd come last. No point in coming in the middle, is there? So where's our prize then?'

The vicar didn't know what to say; he just chuckled nervously. Mike came over waving his trophy under my nose. While he was talking he kept raising his eyebrows and giving me these looks: half-puzzled, half-amused. He wanted to know what I was doing with the Smurf. Sarah must have seen him. The next thing I knew she'd gone.

I saw her standing by the refreshment tent. Everyone was jostling about laughing and talking. Except Sarah. I kept watching her. I was sure she'd take one of those little paper plates and fill it up with food. But she didn't. She just stood there. No-one spoke to her. No-one even seemed to notice her. I thought, she'll slip off home soon.

Then I realized something funny: I didn't want her to go home.

I pushed my way over to the refreshment tent. I grabbed two paper plates right away and piled on as much food as I could on each one. Then I found Sarah. She was still standing on the edge of the refreshment area.

'You're hungry,' she quipped, when she saw me with two plates of food. I didn't actually look at her. I just pointed one of the plates in her direction.

'Is that for me?' She seemed amazed as if I was giving her a plateful of money. 'But I'm not hungry.'

'Go on, take it,' I muttered. She did, and just about scoffed the lot.

Then she told me she'd never been to the park before. I couldn't believe that. So I showed her round. We stayed until it started to rain again.

It was after three o'clock when we set off home.

'You want to get yourself a proper bike, Sarah,' I said.

'I like this one.'

'Behave.'

'I think having a basket is very useful.'

I shook my head. 'You're crazy.'

'So are you.'

'That's true . . . shame you never got a chance to use your first-aid kit, isn't it?' Her face reddened. 'No sign of the ghost today.' Sarah didn't say anything, just went even redder. I couldn't help rubbing it in. 'Just think, if I hadn't punched that ghost he'd still be here now messing about, causing more chaos.'

'You still shouldn't have done it,' said Sarah.

'Can't admit you're wrong, can you?'

'That's because I'm not,' said Sarah, tossing her head defiantly.

I laughed mockingly. After which I decided I'd done enough crowing for now – and changed the subject.

By the time we reached my house the rain was falling really heavily. 'Do you want to

come in for a Coke . . . then when the rain's stopped we can go round Grandad's?'

Sarah looked surprised at the invitation, then she actually gave me a tiny smile.

'No-one's at home, but I've got a key,' I said, airily. I dug into my pocket. I felt for the key.

It wasn't there.

'The key's gone!' I cried. 'My mum'll kill me.'

I could already see my mum's anxious, disappointed face. And my sister just gloating with pleasure. 'I've got to find it, Sarah,' I said. 'But it could be anywhere. It must be back at the park.'

Sarah considered. 'No, it'll be nearer than that. You probably lost it when you fell off your bike.'

'I didn't fall off my bike,' I replied indignantly. 'But you could be right. It's probably just by the dead man's hand. Anyway, I'd better go. I'll give you a ring when I get back.'

'I'm coming with you,' said Sarah.

'But you hate cycling.'

'That's true, but four eyes are better than two, aren't they? We'll find it all right.'

'We'd better,' I replied.

CHAPTER FIFTEEN

The moment we set off the weather turned nasty. That's how it seemed anyway. The wind certainly picked up, driving the rain straight into our faces. I wanted to close my eyes. But I daren't. It was hard enough seeing anything with my eyes open.

This was a bad time for a journey. I wouldn't have set out at all if it hadn't been for Rachel. I just couldn't face her if I'd lost the key. I'd rather leave home.

This was all her fault.

Sarah was crouched over the handlebars, gasping every time the rain smacked her in the face.

'Soon be at Frizzle Wood now,' I called. But the wind whipped my words away.

Then I nearly missed the turning. We swerved into it, earning an irate purp from a car.

'I can't believe how dark it's got in the wood,' said Sarah.

I nodded in agreement. I felt as if we were going down a long tunnel. 'We'll probably see more on foot,' I suggested. We clambered off our bikes and squelched our way through the mud. There were massive puddles everywhere.

Was my key drowning in one of them? It had to be.

Low-lying clouds circled above us. The wind made the trees rattle and shake.

'Look out for the old oak tree,' I cried to Sarah. And before I'd finished speaking I spotted it in the distance. Something else, too.

The dead man's hand.

Only this time it seemed to be waving at us, urging us forward.

'There it is,' I cried. I felt excited, hopeful.

'The key's got to be there. Come on.'

'You go on ahead,' croaked Sarah. 'I'll catch you up.' Rain was dripping off her. She looked as if she was about to fall down.

'Yeah, sure,' I replied, sloshing towards the tree. Then I crouched down. I felt like an explorer searching for a very rare creature. Where was it? I squinted up my eyes.

Out of nowhere came this blast of cold air. It was just as if someone had opened a giant freezer. I could feel it pouring on to my neck. Then something came crashing down on my left shoulder. An icy hand. The next moment another hand gripped my right shoulder. This felt so cold I yelled out. I tried to turn round. I couldn't move. Someone was stopping me.

I couldn't see anyone.

Yet someone was there all right.

It was him.

I struggled frantically, getting more and

more desperate. But I couldn't move. I was caught in some kind of invisible trap. I'd have to stay like this until he decided to let me go.

I let out another cry. I was terrified. All at once Sarah's face loomed up next to mine. Her eyes were like saucers.

'What's happened, Alfie?' she gasped.

'I can't move. It's holding me back.'

'What is?'

'He is. The ghost's here,' I began. Then I let out another cry. Two chilled hands were pressing down even harder on my shoulders now. 'It's come to get me, Sarah,' I gasped, 'just like you said. Run away before it gets you.'

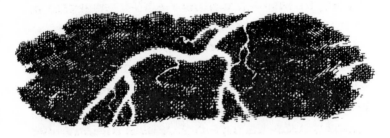

'No, I can't leave you like this,' she began. 'Look, I'll pull it off you.'

She bent down beside me. She was breathing really hard, as if she'd just been running in a race.

I was ice-cold from head to toe now. 'I don't

think you can do a thing,' I began, my teeth chattering, 'but try, anyway.'

'Of course I will,' she began. But before she could do anything there came this great, blinding flash of light. The shock of it made us both fall back on to the mud. I'd always thought lightning was white. But this was electric blue and brighter than the sun. It came racing across the sky. I could see it stretching and growing before it shot down the oak tree: a jagged line of blue fire. There was a great shower of sparks. All at once the earth around us began to shake. Then came this tremendous crack of thunder. The noise ripped through my eardrums while everything around me seemed to be spinning.

I grabbed hold of Sarah's hand or she grabbed hold of mine. I don't remember exactly. And it was hard to make out anything because these little silver flashes kept jumping about in front of my eyes. It was like my own private firework display. I had this prickling sensation. My hair was standing on end.

Then I heard these crackling sounds. They were all around us. It was like hundreds of gunshots going off all at once. Leaves and branches were shooting everywhere; Sarah let go of my hand. I twisted my head round. She was shaking.

'Are you all right?' she asked.

'Yes, I think so.' I suddenly realized I could move my neck again. It ached like crazy, though. 'How about you?'

'Oh, I'm OK,' she said. She'd wrapped both her arms around herself but she was still shaking.

I said, 'I feel like I'm in a war zone somewhere, with guns going off all around me.'

'That's just the branches hitting the ground.'

'I know,' I said quickly. I sniffed. I could smell burning. 'I don't think we're in exactly the safest spot here, do you? We should go.'

'Yes,' agreed Sarah. 'Only my bones feel very heavy at the moment.'

'That's OK,' I said. 'My bones feel pretty heavy too.' There was silence for several moments. Finally, I said, 'I suppose if I'd been under the tree I'd be burnt to a crisp now, wouldn't I?'

'You certainly would.'

'Only he stopped me. I could feel him pressing dead hard on my shoulders, like he was pulling me back. He's got a mighty strong grip for a ghost.' I gave a scratchy kind of laugh. 'He did it, Sarah, he saved me . . . but why?'

She gave an exasperated sigh: the kind contestants on game shows give when they've made a silly mistake. 'I should have realized,' she murmured.

'Realized what?'

She went into her sighing routine again, then she said softly, 'But he's your time-twin.'

'So?'

'So he knew you were in danger. Don't you see, he crossed another dimension to try and warn you.'

A shiver ran through me. 'Only Alfred couldn't get me to understand and I punched him in the face. I really thought he'd vanished for good then.'

'But he was there at your side all the time,' said Sarah. 'You just never knew it.'

There was another rumble of thunder, but it

was a pretty distant one. The thunder was far away now. And Alfred, was he far away now too?

At last we hauled ourselves up out of the mud. My trousers clung to me like freshly hung wallpaper. The rain was stopping and there was this deathly hush. Not a bird for miles around.

This massive, great burn mark was grooved all the way down the oak tree. It was as if it had been split in two.

I thought again of what would have happened to me if I'd been underneath that tree. I stared down at all the dead branches and leaves. They lay everywhere, like the casualties of a battle.

'In the end,' said Sarah, as if reading my thoughts, 'all those branches and leaves will melt into the earth to feed new trees.' Then she sprang forward. There, splattered with mud, was the dead man's hand. She crouched down. Surely she wasn't going to pick it up, I thought. But she'd spotted something else lying beside it. She held it up triumphantly. 'This is your key, isn't it?'

'It has to be,' I said. 'Will you keep hold of it?'

'Yes, it'll be safe with me.'

I shook my head. 'What a day. Now all we've got to do is get back before my mum. She'll go ape if she sees us like this. You can borrow some of my sister's clothes,' I went on.

'Won't she mind?'

'She won't even notice. She's got two wardrobes full of them. Some dresses she only wears once . . . so you might as well use them.'

'Well it would be handy if I could borrow something. My mum would only worry if she saw me like this.'

We fell on to our bikes. How we got home I don't know. But we did – just as Mum was drawing up in her car.

CHAPTER SIXTEEN

Mum looked at us as if she couldn't believe what she was seeing.

'But what are you doing out in the rain? The race finished hours ago – and why are you both covered in mud?'

Sarah and I just hung our heads in reply.

'And Sarah, I'm really surprised at you,' exclaimed Mum. 'I thought you were sensible.' Sarah's head was so low now it was almost touching the ground. 'Well, you can't go home like that. Your mum would have a fit.'

Mum bundled us both inside. She sent Sarah upstairs to have a bath. I had to wait downstairs in my dressing-gown, while Mum had another go at me. 'Honestly, Alfie, you could both have caught your death of cold. You just don't think, do you? And if you get ill who'll have to stay at home and look after you? Me. That's who.' She stopped. She looked at me a bit more gently. 'What happened, then?'

'Nothing.'

'But when I saw you, you both looked scared out of your wits.'

'So we were, we were scared of you, Mum.'

'Oh, come on.'

I smiled a half-smile. 'You wouldn't believe me, Mum,' I murmured.

'What's that?'

I looked up. 'We just forgot about the time, that's all.'

'I see,' said Mum in a tone which suggested she didn't. 'By the way, in all the fuss, I forgot

to ask how you got on in the race?'

I gave another half-smile. 'We came last, actually.'

Next it was my turn to have a bath. I sat staring out of the window thinking about all that had happened.

Afterwards I saw Sarah in the hallway; she'd just been ringing her mum. She looked funny, as she was wearing one of my sister's old jerseys and a pair of my jeans. I really wanted to talk to her. But I couldn't, not with my mum buzzing about.

Mum had cooked us a meal. Neither of us could eat much. I still felt churned up inside. Then the doorbell rang twice. It sounded urgent.

It was Grandad with Molly. I heard him say to Mum: 'Come on, we're going for a walk.' Grandad sounded really excited.

'But it's raining, Dad,' replied Mum.

'Oh, it's stopped now. So come on, stir your stumps, I've got a surprise for you all. Or rather Molly has.'

He breezed past Mum and put his head round the kitchen door: 'Oh good, Sarah is here too,' he rubbed his hands together. 'That's just perfect.'

Mum joined him. 'Well, off you go then. I think these two could do with cheering up. But please don't let them get all muddy again – I'll have a pot of tea waiting for when you get back.'

'But you've got to come too,' said Grandad, firmly.

'I have?' Mum looked stunned.

'Yes,' said Grandad. 'Why, you haven't been out with Molly since she got wheels, have you?'

Mum looked guilty. And then she came with us. I kept asking Grandad what he was up to, but he only laughed mysteriously in reply.

Outside felt fresh, as if it had just been washed clean. It was still very windy though, and drops of water fell off the leaves. But Molly bounced along beside us so confident and happy that even Mum noticed the change in her.

'You haven't seen anything yet,' said Grandad.

'Have you taught Molly some new tricks?' I asked.

'Wait and see,' replied Grandad.

I began to feel a bit peeved. Up to now I'd been the one who'd taught Molly all her tricks. What trick had Grandad taught Molly without me?

We reached the common. To my surprise

Grandad let Molly off the lead. She seemed to hesitate. 'It's all right, girl, off you go,' whispered Grandad. She ran off a little way then came right back. A few seconds later she was off again. Then all at once she was tearing around that common barking in delight, just like any other dog.

'Just look at her,' said Sarah proudly.

Grandad gave a deep sigh of satisfaction. 'She can go anywhere now . . . the world's her oyster.'

'You've certainly done wonders with that dog,' said Mum to Grandad.

'Couldn't have done it without those two,' replied Grandad. Sarah and I tried to look modest.

Molly bounded over to us again as if to check we were still there. Then she was off again, only this time she ran right to the edge of the common which led on to the back of the church. The next moment she'd disappeared through the gate and was speeding off into the church-yard.

'Oh, look where she's gone – will you two go and get her?' asked Grandad.

Sarah and I sprinted off after her. I reached Molly first. She was sniffing excitedly around one of the gravestones.

'Molly, here girl.'

But Molly just wagged her tail at me and went on sniffing. She was acting as if she'd found something amazing.

She had.

I saw it hanging over the gravestone.

I rubbed my eyes.

It was still there.

My black bomber jacket.

I crouched down beside it while Molly bounded around me. I still couldn't believe it.

I had to check it really was my jacket.

I opened up the inside pocket on the right side. That was where I'd let Mum sew the cotton label with my name on.

There it was.

ALFIE DRAYTON.

But how had the jacket got here?

I knelt down beside the grave. It was very

neglected. The inscription was blurred. I looked more closely: IN LOVING MEMORY OF ALFRED GODDARD, WHO DIED ON OCTOBER 29TH 1967, AGED TEN YEARS.

'Alfred,' I whispered. 'Of course. You left it here for me, didn't you?' And as I spoke I felt something brush past my face. It was the lightest of touches. It could just have been a little breeze. But I knew it wasn't. It was Alfred. His one last message for me. I thought I understood this one. He was going away now. But I didn't want him to.

'Alfred,' I called. 'Don't go yet.'

But the only reply was Sarah's: 'Your jacket – is that your jacket?' She was out of breath.

'It is. Molly found it.'

'Clever, clever girl,' said Sarah, rubbing Molly's head. 'But how did it get here?'

Then I let Sarah read the inscription on the gravestone. She stared and stared at it.

'Alfred was here, too. I felt him rush past me,' I said at last.

'Is he still here?' asked Sarah eagerly.

'I'm pretty certain he's not. That was what he wanted to tell me. Well he's done what he wanted to do, hasn't he?'

Sarah nodded. 'Poor Alfred, he tried so hard to help you.'

'I know, I know.' I felt a bit defensive. 'But it's hard enough understanding humans sometimes – never mind ghosts.'

'I wonder what Alfred was like when he was alive?' asked Sarah. She didn't wait for me to answer. 'I think Alfred was very shy, you know, and very lonely too.' She turned away, and she was speaking so softly I had to lean forward. 'He was lonely when he was alive, and he still is now. He finds it very hard to communicate – and yet he wants to so much.' Her voice started to shake. 'I wish he'd stayed here a bit longer.'

'I'll miss him as well,' I said. 'Just when I was getting to understand him too. But anyway *I'm* still around.' I gave a kind of laugh. Then I reached out my hand to her. Sarah half-turned round. She looked at me, then took my hand. She held it tightly.

'Hey,' I said, 'you've got nearly as strong a grip as Alfred.'

She gave me one of her flickering smiles. Then we spotted Grandad and Mum coming over to us.

Grandad recognized the name on the tombstone. 'That was the boy Mrs Porter mentioned, wasn't it?'

'Yes, Grandad, it was.' I put the jacket on again. I remembered the smell of it. How big it felt. Then I noticed something else: it was bone-dry.

'But how did it get here?' asked Mum.

'There's a story about all this, isn't there?' said Grandad.

'Quite a long story, actually,' said Sarah.

'I think it's time we heard it, don't you?' said Grandad.

I looked at Sarah. She nodded. We went back to Grandad's. He made us tea and toast, then we sat by the fire and I told the story I've just been telling you. Only Sarah kept interrupting me. But I didn't mind. This was a special story and every bit had to be right.

Mum and Grandad didn't interrupt once. They just sat there, their faces half in shadow. After we'd finished I said, 'And that's our story. So what do you think, do you believe in ghosts now, Grandad?'

Grandad stirred his tea thoughtfully; he hadn't drunk it once while we'd been talking. 'It's a good yarn, I'll give you that.'

'But do you believe it really happened?' asked Sarah.

'I know you two believe it,' said Grandad. He was smiling now.

'But what about you?' I persisted.

Grandad sat back in his chair. 'I'll tell you this; I'd like to believe it was true.'

'Of course it's true Grandad,' I exclaimed. 'If it hadn't been for Alfred I'd be toast now.'

'But I know it's hard for older people to understand things like this,' said Sarah kindly. 'My great-grandad didn't believe men would ever walk on the moon, not even when he saw them on television.'

We turned towards Mum. She didn't say much at all.

But next day we asked Mum if we could borrow the clippers as Sarah and I wanted to get rid of the weeds on Alfred's grave, and to my surprise she came with us. She even stopped off at the florist shop and bought a bunch of chrysanthemums.

Much later I went back to Alfred's grave with Molly. It was grey-dark now and there was no-one about, just a few birds twittering drowsily. I knelt down and Molly snuggled up next to me, her head warm on my knee.

If only Alfred hadn't left so fast. I wondered how far away he was, and whether he could still hear me. Probably not. But just in case, I whispered, 'Alfred, just to let you know, you won't see a single weed on your grave again. Sarah and I will see to that. And . . . I'm really sorry I punched you in the face.'

I got up and Molly and I began to walk away. But then I turned back and called into the darkness, 'I'll never forget what you did for me, Alfred. NEVER.'

THE END

SOME THINGS YOU MAY NOT KNOW ABOUT PETE JOHNSON:

- He used to be a film critic on Radio One. Sometimes he saw three films a day.

- He has met a number of famous actors and directors, and collects signed film pictures.

- Pete's favourite book when he was younger was *One Hundred and One Dalmations*. Pete wrote to the author of this book, Dodie Smith. She was the first person to encourage Pete to be a writer. *Traitor* is dedicated to her.

- Once when Pete went to a television studio to talk about his books he was mistaken for an actor and taken to the audition room. TV presenter Sarah Greene also once mistook Pete for her brother.

- When he was younger Pete used to sleepwalk regularly. One night he woke up to find himself walking along a busy road in his pyjamas.

- Pete's favourite food is chocolate. He especially loves Easter eggs and received over forty this year.

- Pete's favourites of his own books are *The Ghost Dog* and *How to Train Your Parents*. The books he enjoys reading most are thrillers and comedies.

- Pete likes to start writing by eight o'clock in the morning. He reads all the dialogue aloud to see if it sounds natural. When he's stuck for an idea he goes for a long walk.

- He carries a notebook wherever he goes. 'The best ideas come when you're least expecting them' he says.

If you ve enjoyed these spooky stories from Pete Johnson,
you might also enjoy his funny books!
Turn the page to read the first chapter of

HOW TO TRAIN YOUR PARENTS

Arriving in Swotsville

I think I've arrived somewhere weird.

Started at my new school today. I was met by this moth-eaten old geezer who said he was the headmaster. He's about a hundred and eight, has one huge eyebrow and spits a lot. Had to wipe my face down after he'd gone. I was soaked through.

He told me four times how lucky I was to come to his school and he kept getting my name wrong. It's Louis, pronounced Lou-ee, not as he said it, Lewis. But I didn't say anything. I was a bit scared of that eyebrow.

Next I met my form teacher, Mr Wormold, a helmet-fringed weasel who

7

said he hoped I'd be a credit to the school, but was already looking distinctly doubtful about this.

Then he introduced me to the class. They all stared at this diddy boy with an onion-shaped head and brown, spiky hair. I got all nervous. Now, whenever I'm nervous I start talking in an Australian accent. So I said to them, 'G'day to you possums.' They just gaped at me in silence.

I sat down next to this boy called Theo. I'd met him briefly the day we moved here. He lives in a massive house at the top of my road.

He asked me if I was really Australian. 'Only in the mornings,' I replied. Not a flicker of a smile crossed his face.

Looking around the classroom I quickly spotted there weren't any girls here (I'm observant like that) and although most girls annoy me I do sort of miss seeing them around the place. Also, there were only twenty pupils in the class and that's not nearly enough. (At my old school there was practically double that number.)

My first lesson was English. The teacher was giving back some projects from last term and the tension was just incredible.

You'd have thought they were all waiting for their lottery results.

Then at break-time, Theo's mobile went off. It was, of all people, his dad. He was ringing to see how Theo had got on with his project. Theo had actually got the best grade in the class, A minus.

'Hearing that will put a smile on my dad's face,' he said proudly.

If my dad rang me at school he wouldn't be smiling for long, I can tell you.

After school Theo had to rush off because of his French horn lesson. Just about everyone else in my class was beetling off for an extra lesson in something gruesome.

Have I landed in Swotsville, dear diary?

TUESDAY JANUARY 8TH

Advantages of moving here:

1) My bedroom hasn't got that funny cheesy smell which my old one had. This is because I don't have to share with a loathsome, whiny midget called Elliot any more.

2) That's it.

Disadvantages of moving here:
1) I wasn't consulted. Last November my relics just announced we're moving closer to London, as Dad had been offered this new job right out of the blue. 'It's the chance of a lifetime,' he announced. 'And at my advanced age too,' he added, as a sort of joke. And that was it. He didn't even bother to ask if I'd mind moving hundreds of miles away.
2) I'd lived at my old house all my life (twelve whole years) and really didn't want to leave.
3) I hated leaving all my old mates behind.
4) Every day at my new school lasts for three centuries.
5) Laughing is against the law there.
6) I'm only at that school because Dad's new boss is very chummy with one of the governors. My parents don't know that I overheard them saying all this.
7) I feel dead lonely.
8) Too depressing to list any more.

WEDNESDAY JANUARY 9TH

The neighbours here are a right misery. After school this afternoon I was playing a game of footie by myself in the back garden, when the woman next door rang up to complain about all the noise I was making. She said I was stopping Olympia from concentrating on her work.

Olympia's five years old!

THURSDAY JANUARY 10TH

Theo's a wet weed.

He always looks as if his parents have just washed and ironed him. And I know he can't help that. But he talks all the time in this quiet, whispery voice, is dead serious about everything and has no sense of humour at all (in other words, he doesn't laugh at any of my jokes).

Some of the other pupils are OK. But everyone here seems so anxious and nervous and kind of damped down all the time. It's as if this school's sucked all the fun out of them. Well, it'd better not try to do the same to me.

11

FRIDAY JANUARY 11TH

I had my first homework back today in science. And straight away, Theo was buzzing in my ear, 'So what did you get then?' as if it really mattered.

I got 10/20 and it's no big deal, so I told him. And he couldn't stop himself from giving this little smile.

Later I spotted him writing down my mark at the back of his exercise book. 'What are you doing that for?' I asked.

He went very red and said, 'My mum really wanted to know.'

I think his mum needs to get out more.

Actually, I'm pretty content with 10/20. I never got massively high marks at my old school either. I'd say I'm average at most things. Maybe a bit above average in public speaking and English (though my spelling is rubbish) and a bit below it in the really evil subjects like French and maths. Up to now, my parents have been fairly happy with my school reports. Teachers usually said I was too gobby but they sort of liked me just the same.

And anyway, I'm not really bothered because school's got absolutely nothing to do with my career. You see, I'm going to be a comedian. Don't laugh. Well, you can if you like. But there's only one thing in the world I can really do well and that's make people grin.

Even when I was about two years old I was making my nan and my aunties laugh. I'd sing silly songs and then, when I was a bit older, tell silly jokes too and do impressions of people off the telly. And my nan would be wiping her eyes saying I was a 'little imp'. And my mum would be declaring she didn't know where I got it from, while I just felt so happy and proud.

At school, too, I was always the one who'd liven up the lessons by saying something daft. In fact, if a lesson was especially boring people would start looking at me to lift their spirits.

Then last year there was this talent show for children. Twenty-three contestants, and the winner was . . . ME. Got the certificate on my bedroom wall to prove it.

Actually, I was dead nervous when I first went out on that stage. My old heart was pumping away and I was sweating buckets . . . and I started burbling away in an Australian accent.

Still not sure if the audience were laughing at my jokes or my terrible accent. But anyway, they were laughing and I felt something click inside me and I wasn't scared any more. In fact, I could have stayed on that stage for much longer. Can't tell you how intoxicating it was. Best moment of my entire life.

SATURDAY JANUARY 12TH

Tonight my family was invited to walk up to the top of the road and hang out at Theo's mansion.

Theo's dad opened the door. 'Welcome aboard,' he bellowed at us. He's as bald as a snooker ball and absolutely massive. He grabbed my hand, crushed it for about two years and when I squeaked, 'Hello, Mr Guerney,' shook his head vigorously and boomed, 'We don't stand on ceremony here! I'm Mike and that's Prue.'

Prue (Theo's mum) was slinking about in these black flowery trousers and jangling like crazy because she was wearing so many bracelets. She said there was masses of food and we must all 'really tuck in', then handed us plates the size of contact lenses.

After the meal came an unexpected cabaret. Theo played the piano (he looked at me and blushed a bit before he started) and then Mike and Prue told us about Theo's many musical accomplishments. Then they went on to recount Theo's many other achievements. But by now I was yawning too loudly to hear properly.

Next it was Theo's sister Libby's turn to entertain. She's only six, the same age as Elliot (as Mum observed in a hushed voice to Dad afterwards), yet she could recite the names of all the kings and queens from 1066 to the present day.

At the end Mum asked, 'But how have they managed to achieve all this so young?'

'Well, they've both got brains like sponges,' cried Mike, 'and are soaking up knowledge all the time, but also . . .' He looked at Prue.

Prue beckoned to us to follow her into the kitchen. On the wall was a chart showing all Theo and Libby's out-of-school activities: music, art appreciation, chess and other equally grisly things were all up there.

'It's hard work keeping up with it all,' said Prue, 'and knowing where I need to be and with what equipment. But we're determined that our two won't squander a second of their time.'

Mum and Dad stared at the chart, goggle-eyed with amazement. Then Elliot piped up that he'd written a story today.

'Oh, do tell us about it, dear,' cooed Prue.

'It's all about this person who eats bogies,' he began.

I caught Mum's eye and saw she was trying very hard not to smile. Shortly afterwards we all tottered out of there. Never to return, I hope.

HOW TO TRAIN YOUR PARENTS 0 440 96439 9

Copyright © Pete Johnson, 2003